Pulp Books is an imprint of Pulp Faction
PO Box 12171, London N19 3HB.
First published by Pulp Books, 1997.
All rights reserved.

A CIP record for this book is available
from the British Library.
ISBN 190107207x

The following extracts appear with
permission:
Bomb Culture by Kirk Lake, from the
album *So you got anything else?*
(Ché Trading 1995)
The Baddest Man on the Planet
by Kirk Lake, from the album *The Black
Lights* (I Records 1996)
Arable Land by Paul Lamont
Lyrics reproduced by kind permission of
Howdy Partners Publishing © 1986.

Cover design: Engine
Author photo: Beverley Marsland

NEVER HIT THE GROUND

KIRK LAKE

<3>

Part One

Easy Baby Easy
A Blue Funk
If Fishes Could Talk
52 Girls
Lisa
Queen Jane Approximately And
Absolutely Sweet Marie
Bomb Culture
Out In The Open
The Baddest Man On The Planet
Any Kind Of Star
Nowhere Fast
1000 Eyes
Class Acts
Goodbye Johnny
Wreckology
Loose Joints
Queerfish
If This Was A Rocketship
No Smoking
Dead Flowers
Sweet Thursday
99.9%
Big Road Blues

Easy Baby Easy

Queen Jane moved slowly among the racks, fingering the jewel cases. Occasionally she would pick up a CD and pretend to study the track-listing while she scanned the store for staff and security. Walking alongside her, close up, was Marie. She'd lean over the Queen and put her arm on her shoulder and they'd talk about the music while, with her free hand, she dropped another CD into the gaping canvas bag at her feet that was partially covered by Queen Jane's coat.

The Queen moved to the end of the rack, where the soundtrack section finished. Marie followed her, a mannered shuffle as she slid the bag along with her feet. She picked up two copies of a double-CD set of Nino Rota themes and handed one to Marie who put it into her jacket pocket. Then Marie kneeled down and zipped up the hold-all, picked it up and followed the Queen to the counter.

The boy at the till had long dreads and was wearing a Thelonius Monk: High Priest Of Bop teeshirt. His ID badge hung from a black bootlace amongst chinking glass beads and drilled silver coins. Queen Jane winked at him as he took her money, and purred a Pleeeased to meet you Edwin. He threw back a quizzical look, leaned over the counter slightly, looked at her. He ran the CD over a raised pad in front of him then dropped it into a plastic bag and handed it to her with her change and receipt.

Marie stood a couple of steps away with the hold-all at her feet and her hands in her pockets. As the Queen turned from the counter Marie took a step to the side so that the Queen walked straight into her. Oh I'm sorry, oh how clumsy. They both laughed. The Queen had dropped the plastic bag and Marie bent to pick it up, No, no let me get it, I'm so sorry. While she kneeled to get the bag Marie swapped the CD from her pocket for the one

<7>

they'd just bought. Even the Queen didn't see her do it and when she took the bag back she had to ask if they were ready to go. Marie nodded, they linked arms and walked towards the exit together.

As they reached the door, Marie gave the Queen's arm a little squeeze and they parted. Before their feet hit the pavement outside, the alarm started ringing and the red lights on top of the chromium pillars on either side of the door flashed. Queen Jane turned around and held up her plastic bag as two security guards ran towards the door.

Oooh I don't know what it is. I just bought this one minute ago. Maybe it's my jewellery, she giggled and rattled the cheap metal bangles on each wrist. She glanced over her shoulder, out into the street. Marie had disappeared into the crowd.

The security guards switched off the alarm and then got Queen Jane to walk back through the door minus the CD. Silence. They took it back up to the counter and the boy in the Monk tee ran it over the pad and handed it back saying, Sorry, I guess this thing ain't working properly. Queen Jane told Edwin not to worry, then apologised for any trouble she might have caused. She walked back out of the store, making sure she wiggled her ass good for all the eyes she knew were on it. Hmmm easy, baby.

<8>

A Blue Funk

Ray yanked at a pull thread on the sofa, following the thread as it puffed out little clouds of dust along the arm until it reached the scratched wooden panel at the front. And, not for the first time in the last three days, he thought about Lisa and he thought about Rudi. Okay, so he'd been holding at Hades, and okay the girl *had* turned blue in the cubicle but what the fuck? Who's to say she wouldn't have keeled on the fat man's shit? And, hey, you can't be held responsible for the weakness of somebody's constitution. So, strictly, he'd been off limits and it had been dumb, but then how could he be sure it had been him anyway? How could Rudi have been so sure? Rudi might have the eye but he couldn't keep it open over all the traffic in the place. Just because he hadn't had the word from the fat man didn't mean he was going to go in there and start selling bad shit.

He didn't remember seeing the girl before. He was certain he hadn't dealt with her personally. Okay, it was hard to tell for sure when she was lying in a pool of urine, shaking horribly, rattling almost, with sick dribbling down her chin onto the tiles of the ladies toilet but... And anyway, Rudi was the fucking psycho. Hadn't he held him over the girl's body screaming, Do you see what you've done... like someone house-training a pet the hard way? Hadn't he made sure to find someone to point the finger at before they'd even called the ambulance?

All that screaming and crying and pointing going on, girls in the toilets pleading, Help her. For god's sake, help her. The phones aren't working. Somebody go outside to the callbox on the corner. The doors are locked, they're not letting anyone out. Help her. Jesus. Help her.

And all the while they were busy finding Ray.

Yeah, he had a yellow teeshirt on. No, no definitely, we bought a couple each. He had a nice smile. Six foot I suppose. Black hair.

<9>

Well it might've been brown. Yeah it was him, that one. Him. Him.

Ray in an Everlast teeshirt, fingered by someone he was sure he'd never seen.

What? Yeah look it's gold. Gold. Not fucking yellow anyway. I don't wear yellow. Yellow? Fuck off man. And Christ anyway, you trust her judgment? She's out of her box man. Fried. Aw Rudi, you're kidding man. I've never even seen her before. Never ever. Well fuck you too.

Even if it had been his stuff, for sure, then if she'd died it would've been Rudi to blame just as much as him. A fifteen minute search before the phone-lines were switched back on to call the ambulance. And anyway, in the end, where was the harm? The girl survived. The fat man wasn't going to lose his licence. By the time the police got there the whole place was clean.

He'd apologised, handed over the rest of his gear. Sure he had. He remembered Rudi's sagging face and cigar breath only inches away from his own, saying, ever so slowly, I will be paid back for this. Don't forget it. You couldn't see around him. Couldn't see anything else. Rudi's bulk, big wide shoulders like BOOM, blackness, the sun's gone out.

And this had been worse than the beating Ray had braced himself for. When they bundled him into the back of the car, the last place he thought they'd take him was home. It could've been a gun stuck in his ribs through the pocket of the bald man's jacket when they marched him up the stairs. He'd thought he'd be lucky to be able to crawl back down but as soon as he handed over the rest of his merchandise from the drawer in the bedroom they'd packed up and gone, leaving him sweating on his own sofa in pretty much the same position he was in now. The guy in the black jacket with the busted nose and cue-ball head had even thrown him a comb on the way out and cackled about how he should clean himself up a little, how he looked a fucking state.

<10>

Adding that Ray would be hearing from Rudi in due course.

If it hadn't been for Lisa he would've split there and then. Of course he'd seen Rudi before, but never up so close, and as the fat man spat threats and insults into his face all Ray could focus on were his teeth, stained, brown and crooked. So crooked that it looked like he had double rows top and bottom, like shark's teeth ready to snap into place as the need arose.

Now he was right back where he started. All those months of scrabbling for funds, the petty little scams and the high risk, low reward jobs were for nothing. He'd turned all that cash into an in-demand product, something that would've provided him and Lisa with the means to get ahead for once, and the first time he took it out on the street he'd lost the fucking lot. Ray sighed and lit up a cigarette. He took a long draw and blew out a train of smoke rings, prodded his finger through the largest of the rings, scattering the smoke. Fuck you, Rudi.

<11>

If Fishes Could Talk

The bones were bleached white. Only the clear resin in which they were encased kept them in some semblance of a hand, fingers spread, the tips pointing upwards, forming a shallow bowl. A fatter, living hand jabbed the glowing tip of a cigar into the place where the flesh of the palm would once have been.

Rudi swivelled in his chair, got up and walked across the office towards the two shelves of fishtanks. From the pocket of his burgundy check jacket, he took a small plastic container, unscrewed the top and took a pinch of its contents between his thumb and index finger. Carefully, he dropped the food into the large tank on the lower shelf. Red and gold fish flashed like balls of fire in the clear water as they twisted and turned to chase the flakes slowly drifting down towards the coloured gravel at the bottom of the tank. Rudi carefully lifted down one of the small tanks from the top shelf. About the size and shape of a large coffee jar, it could comfortably be held in one hand. He held it up in front of him. Caught in the light from the desk lamp was a single, dull brown fish a little over two inches long. Rudi peered in at the fish and tapped the glass. The fish swam around a little, opening and closing its mouth. Rudi mimicked it, showing off teeth that were as brown as the fish. He set the tank down on his desk and pressed his intercom.

Frank. Get a message to that guy we pulled in here. Yeah, that Ray Gardner. Tell him I want to see him. Tomorrow. Tell him I have a little errand for him to run.

Rudi sat at his desk and stared at the fish. It swam around in a tight circle, then stared back, opening and closing its mouth.

<12>

52 Girls

Ray sipped from a bottle of Jolt cola and flipped 52 girls, one after the other, head over heels across the room. He pointed his finger like the barrel of a pink handgun and cocked his thumb. Okay, pull! KAPOW! POW! POW! He let out a whistle as one of the girls tumbled through the air and dropped into the grey felt hat in front of the muted TV. Ray flipped another card, aimed and fired. POW! POW! It spun off sideways and disappeared behind a cardboard box of books. Winged the fucker. Haha. He blew imaginary smoke from the tip of his finger.

Ray looked at the phone. He could make a call, start up on an upfront riff that'd blow the fat guy away. Hey, fat guy! Yeah I know what I'm saying. I said fat guy. Fat-fucking-lard-fucking-guy. So what's happening? What are you gonna do? Because if you're gonna do nothing then I guess I may as well say seeyoulater and start moving. You don't get nowhere by letting the grass grow under your feet and you know I've got things to do, I've got plans so if you're not gonna stand in my way then I'll start rolling them now.

Yeah, he could. Only thing was, he didn't have a plan. He'd been sitting here for three days waiting for some stroke of genius to come crashing down on his head but nothing was happening. Genius wouldn't deal him in. So he'd wait for Rudi to get in touch. Wait for that fat fucker to call him in.

It was like he told Lisa last time he saw her, You know, my life is like those talk-shows you cut into when you're flicking through the channels on the car radio. You hear these people, you understand the words but you can't make out the point. Then, just as you're getting a handle on it, you drive through a tunnel or pass under a railway bridge and the signal disappears and by the time you get out in the open you're lost again. Well I must've

<13>

stalled my car under the bridge baby, because I sure as fuck don't know what's happening now.

Ray looked at the TV, some lurid musical from the 40s. A show-stopping dance number in which a group of sailors were two-stepping some grass-skirted island girls. Miles blew *Autumn Leaves* around the room and the cassette player's tiny red LED indicators swayed in time with the music. A shaft of late afternoon sunlight spilled through the gap in the curtains and dust danced to the trumpet.

Ray drained the cola bottle and dropped it onto a pile of papers and magazines by the arm of the sofa. He gathered the playing cards from the floor then fanned them out. Pasties, G-strings, peroxide blondes and pneumatic brunettes in showgirl lingerie. Ray shuffled the deck, the eight of spades rising to the top—a red-headed cowgirl, pouting, flourished a pistol in each hand, naked under a fringed leather waistcoat and chaps. He held the eight between the tips of two fingers and flicked it across the room, watching it skim over the hat, flip against the TV screen and drop to the floor. He set the rest of the pack down on the arm of the sofa and went into the kitchen.

Pigeons flapped and scraped across a skylight set in the angled ceiling, its glass obscured by grey and black pigeon shit. Pacing again. Pacing backwards, forwards, backwards, forwards. Living room. Kitchen. Living room. Kitchen. Bedroom. Living room bedroom kitchen. Padding around like some sad big cat in the zoo. Shit. Oh, genius muse come crack me across the skull. Kitchen.

Even at this hour he had to pull the cord to see properly. Bare bulb. A couple of flies worrying it. Some kind of fur growing on the flex and up around the ceiling rose. The wallpaper nicotine yellow and bubbling from the damp or hanging in strips. Over the worst patch, Ray had hung a painting he'd got from a guy who'd owed him and claimed to be an artist. Ray agreed to take the

<14>

painting in lieu of the money before he'd actually seen the thing. He just liked the idea of owning a painting but... It may as well have been a mirror. A two foot by three oil of a room as drab and run down as Ray's kitchen. The artist's own room, one of a series. These days, Ray was told in a slit-eyed, red-eyed, lazy mumbling drawl by some bullshitting boho he dealt with, these days the artist only painted the interference off TV sets. Like, *this is art man, I'm tellin' ya, y'gotta hold on to that painting because this guy is going to be hanging up there with the best of them. A Pollock for the global village. These paintings are like religious icons, TV is the new god, right, and this guy is the only artist addressing that right now. He's hip to it.* Yeah, fuck. Like paintalongwithnancylobotomy real time. Still, Ray wished he'd got one of those instead. It would be like having an extra TV in the house. Hell, he could have had three and had a set in every room. Would've been funnier at the very least.

Ray stripped the cellophane off a new pack of cigarettes and turned on the gas ring. Hand on his forehead to stop his fringe flopping into the blue flame, he inhaled, held it and then blew out the smoke with force. This waiting was driving him crazy. He'd hoped that by giving himself a couple of days clear he'd come up with a way of getting ahead, getting Lisa, and going. Only thing was how. He'd been almost there. Almost. He pinched the air in front of his face. That fucking close.

The cassette player clicked off as the tape ended and an orchestral theme was just audible from the muted TV set. The credits were rolling as he walked back into the room. He knelt in front of a wooden crate on the floor beneath the window. Cigarette dangling from his mouth, he sifted through the box of loose cassettes, screwing up his face as the smoke curled into his eyes. Ray dropped the Miles Davis album into the crate with a clatter, then slotted another tape into the machine and turned up the volume until the speakers hissed in anticipation. A holler, and

<15>

the Wolf was howlin' for his baby. Ray did the slow shuffle back to the sofa, sliding his feet across the carpet, knees bent, cigarette held out in front of him like a midget partner and then growling with the Wolf at the end of the line, *Lord have mercy, darrrrlinnnng!* Ray searched out the TV remote from under a sofa cushion and began flicking through the channels. Shouting at the TV screen. Shit number one. Shit number two. Horses, fuck the fuckin' horses. Three was a gameshow. The host, in an electric blue suit and a tartan bow-tie, looked as if he was made of plastic. Pretty excitable though and, when a long blonde-haired girl wheeled on a canteen of cutlery in a wooden case, he was as good as running on the spot. Christ, the girl was even more plastic than he was, better watch herself under those studio lights, a real doll, right down to the painted smile. The contestant looked confused and the host put his arms around her and gave her an 'it's alright' hug, nearly lifting her off her feet. Ray leaned forward, Don't listen to him, TAKE THE FUCKIN' MONEY!!! The camera zoomed in on the host and his mouth slipped into sync with the singing still roaring out of the tape machine. This was good. Such a thin, weedy guy miming to the Wolf. Ray laughed out loud then screamed at the set again, Take the fuckin' money, ha ha!

Over the sound of his laughing and the music, the telephone rang. Once. Twice. Let it ring. Four times. Ray tried to concentrate on the TV as the contestant was shut into a booth with headphones on and a clock appeared at the bottom of the screen. He watched the seconds count down on the screen. Six times. Seven times. Is it now? I guess this is 'in due course'. Eight times. JESUS CHRIST ALMIGHTY... OKAY OKAY.

He dug into the mess of paper by the sofa and uncovered the phone. He carried it over to the window and after the tenth ring he picked it up.

YEAH?

Ray? Ray, that you?

<16>

Yeah, Lisa. It's me. Who'd you think it was going to be?

Ray turned off the cassette player and pulled back the curtains a little. Down on the street, three floors below, shoppers crowded the entrance to the indoor market, traffic crawled one car-length at a time, drivers hitting their horns and scattering flustered pedestrians as they weaved their way across the road.

Alright Ray, yeah... anyway, where've you been? You said you'd phone days ago and I...

Yeah, but I said for you not to...

Call. Yeah, I know. But I was getting worried. I thought you'd gone and disappeared. Left me for someone else.

Lisa baby. You know there just isn't any hope of that.

So what's happening then. Up there jazzin' yourself is my guess. Hey Ray? Lisa laughed.

No. I've been growing a beard. Ray ran his fingers over his chin.

Well you act like a cunt...

So I may as well look like one. Yeah, very funny Lisa. You're a comic. You know that? A fuckin' comedian.

On TV the gameshow was finishing, everyone upstage waving as tinsel fell over the studio. It was good to hear Lisa's voice again. Maybe he'd been over reacting. Maybe this locking himself away wasn't the answer. He sure as hell hadn't come up with a plan and it wasn't as if Rudi didn't know how to find him. Who was he trying to fool? If something was going to happen it wouldn't make any odds how long he shut himself away. If it was coming, it was coming and there wasn't one damn thing he could do about it. Ray rubbed at a smear on the red plastic telephone, digging it away with his fingernail.

Look baby, sorry I haven't called but things are just a little, uh, complicated at the moment and I didn't want you mixed up in it.

Why? What's happening? Tell me. Lisa's voice was more pleading than demanding.

<17>

Are you calling from work?

Yeah.

What time do you finish? I could meet you later. I'll tell you all about it then.

Well, I'm supposed to finish up in about an hour but, y'know he sacked the other waitress right? It's just been me here all day. It's driving me crazy and my feet are killing me and he just sits out the back all day drinking. So like, not only do I have to take the orders and get the drinks but I'm having to cook the food too. And every time I go in the kitchen he makes a grab for me. Fuckin' creep. I was going to call you earlier but this was the first chance I got.

Outside, two policemen were chasing a young boy who was dodging in and out of the pedestrians, zig-zagging through traffic across the road. An elderly man held out his walking stick and the boy went sprawling to the pavement.

Ray smiled. Well I told you what to do about Doctor Octopus. Remember?

Yeah Ray, I know. I just don't know if I can.

Oh come on. You can. It'll work.

Okay, okay. We'll see. Now, I've got to go and clean this place up or I'll never get away. What are we doing about tonight?

How about we just meet up at the usual place and then you can take it from there. I'll leave it all up to you.

Alright. About nine?

Nine's okay with me. See you then.

Yeah and Ray… whatever it is. Don't worry.

Ray cut the connection and blew a kiss into the handset which he set down on the floor, leaving it purring into the carpet.

On the street, the police were french-walking the boy towards a squad car. A crowd gathered as the boy was bundled into the back seat. Ray glanced at his wristwatch and turned the tape machine back on.

<18>

Lisa

Lisa hung up and waited for the unused coins to drop from the payphone. She smiled at herself as she passed the mirror behind the bar, the smile quickly vanishing as she heard a roar from the kitchen.

You finished cleaning up out there yet Leezer?

Lisa leaned through the serving hatch that connected the kitchen with the bar area and shouted that she was not finished cleaning up, that she hadn't even started and that her name was not fuckin' Leezer. Like when he grabbed her whispering, Hey Leezer the pleezer I'm gonna squeeze yer, and laughing, tongue flopping, dribbling. Mmmmm I'm going to squeeeze you. Huh? Maybe Ray was right and it was time to get the bastard. He certainly made her mad enough to try.

She moved quickly over to the tables and started to clear them. The men had left a pile of coins, hidden by a red paper napkin. As Lisa stacked the crumb covered plates and screwed up the used napkins, she knocked the coins from the table sending them spinning across the floor. Jesus. Not only do I have to serve the pigs but I have to clean up after them too. Kneeling on the stone floor, Lisa gathered up a handful of small change. A few odd coins had run under a table across the room but she couldn't be bothered to crawl around after them. She counted the money in her hand. A pitiful sum. After they'd been trying to cop a feel of her all afternoon, stinking out the place with cheap cigars and bad jokes. She gathered up the rest of the plates and glasses, all the while cursing business lunches and thanking Christ that it was, at last, afternoon closing time and all the toads had crawled back to hassle their secretaries after hours or headed home to fall asleep at the table in front of their wives' oh-so-lovingly prepared meals.

Gerard, the bar owner, a blue striped apron straining to cover

<19>

his belly, was sitting drinking red wine beside the open door to the alleyway. He coughed and spat a ruby red gob onto the stack of crushed vegetable boxes outside the door and turned to face Lisa as she entered from the bar carrying the tray of glasses and plates. He had fired the cook, claiming that he could do better himself and had sacked the other waitress when she asked for more money. He said that he was careful but Lisa called it something else. Careful? When it came to passing out money, Gerard was constipated. The two months that Lisa had been working there had seen G's Spot slump from being a neat little bar-restaurant to a place where businessmen drank up their expense accounts and the food was mere table dressing. Now it was left to Lisa to run the whole show, taking orders, serving drinks and clearing tables. Gerard was supposed to manage everything else and, of course, he couldn't. As the days dragged on he'd sit looking out the back door, drinking away the afternoon with a bottle of house red or white and whining about his wife having left him and the fact that it was she that had driven him to go out and look for other women and that she had a damned nerve to throw him out of their house, no his house, when he got pulled for kerb-crawling by an undercover policewoman. Lisa was left making apologies to customers about the interminable delay in their orders and serving drinks on the house to placate the most vociferous complainants.

She dropped the tray onto the draining board. Barking: Listen Gerard. If you don't get me some help out there I'm quitting.

He stood, poured some wine into an unwashed glass and held it out to her. Leezer, Leezer. Okay, I'll find someone. It's so hard to get good people. Someone like you, he leered and took a swig from the glass that Lisa had refused. You did well today. Is that everybody out? Everybody happy?

Yeah. The last bunch of suits just left and I've put up the closed sign. I'm just clearing the tables. I know it's your place and

<20>

everything but if you don't at least wash up the plates then there's nothing for me to serve up on and if you don't even attempt to prepare the orders then I might just as well tell people that the kitchen is closed and save everybody the aggravation and… Lisa in full flow, hands on hips …If you don't get somebody to help me run the bar then you're not going to have any customers left. No one wants to wait fifteen minutes for a drink and Christ only knows what you do, or how you manage when I'm not here.

Through his wine haze, Gerard began to sense Lisa's agitation. Hey, calm down. Tonight we stay closed. I have some business to attend to. You take the night off. I'll still pay you of course. Now how about a little drink? He offered the glass of wine to her again but she turned her back on him and started to fill a wire tray with steaming glasses from the dishwasher.

Don't do me any favours, hey? Tonight's my night off anyway. Now take that dirty stuff from the draining board and put it in here, she gestured to the empty dish-washer, I don't want to hang around here a minute longer than I have to.

Lisa backed out of the door with the tray of clean glasses and carried them over to the bar. There was a knocking on the glass of the front door and she glanced over to see two men rattling the handle, pointing at her.

We're closed, are you fucking blind? She pointed at the sign hanging against the glass. The men shrugged their shoulders and tried the door again. Lisa gave them the finger and walked behind the counter.

With a green and white checked cloth, Lisa began to polish the glasses and hang them by their stems or handles on a notched wooden rail above the spirits shelf. She started up humming a little tune that had been running around in her head, chasing after the melody, trying to place the words or where it had come from. Refrain. Another snatch, stumbling into a song. She started singing, softly. Gerard had followed her through from the kitchen

<21>

and was now standing behind her, leaning over the bar to look at her legs, her dress inching shorter up her thighs as she stretched on tip-toes to hang the glasses. She stopped singing.

Don't think I don't know what you're doing Gerard.

Gerard walked around the bar until he stood directly behind her. You're a very beautiful girl. Maybe you'd like to come back to my flat for a drink and I can, uh, show you how much I appreciate everything you've done for me. He brushed his hand against Lisa as he slurred his way to the end of the sentence.

Okay Ray, this is it. She wished she'd let Ray tell her exactly what the girl had done, but she'd always figured she'd never really try. But today. Today she was just pissed off enough to try anything. She turned around to face Gerard and smiled, toying with the top button of her dress.

Well Gerard, maybe we could just have a little drink here. I mean, now everybody's gone home and... She gave a little wink, nauseating herself with the sweet little girl voice she was using ...It's just us.

Oh Leezer. Gerard lurched forward grabbing her with both hands, Let me kiss you Leezer. I knew we could be friends. Lisa stood her ground as he ran his hands roughly over her breasts and reached beneath her dress to her ass. Leering forward with vinegar breath he pressed his mouth up to hers murmuring, Leezer, oh Leezer the pleezer.

She could taste the wine on his lips and his tongue felt rough and cold. With one sharp movement Lisa brought her knee up to his groin, feeling his balls squash on contact and folding him in half with a gasp. Lisa ran to the end of the bar and grabbed her bag from a shelf beneath the counter. As Gerard stumbled towards her she pressed the No Sale button on the till and grabbed all the notes she could from the drawer. She picked up a bottle of red wine from the shelf above the till and held it out like a club in front of her.

<22>

Get out of my fuckin' way. So help me. Swinging the bottle, Lisa barged past the stunned owner and ran to the front door. And listen to me Gerard. If you make a complaint or try and raise any sort of fuss at all then I'll tell them you tried to molest me. Okay, you sad fucker?

Gerard, still doubled up and gasping for air, could only raise his head and watch as Lisa let herself out of the door and into the street. After a few seconds, he heard a crash as the wine bottle came spiralling through the window, showering the tables with glass, then shattering itself and spilling foaming red liquid over the stone floor.

<23>

Queen Jane Approximately And Absolutely Sweet Marie

They had a big pile of CDs on the table. Laughing and peeling off the wrappers, reading the sleeve notes.

Oh isn't he just adorable? I mean really. Look at him. Jane unfolded the booklet and pushed it across the table.

Yeah, but his sounds are shit. Truly. Marie picked up the booklet. Watch it you're getting beer all over them.

The Queen took a sip from her drink and wiped the base of her glass with her hand before she put it back down. What are we going to do with all these anyway? You picked some real lemons here. Look at this one. She pulled a CD out of the pile and showed it to Marie. We're not going to be able to sell this thing to anyone. Who'd want it? Couldn't even give it away.

Marie took the CD and put it back in the bag then took the stack from the table and dropped them in on top of it. Yeah, I know. But I got what I could. Someone will buy them.

Absolutely Sweet Marie walked over to the bar and ordered a couple more. Queen Jane Approximately sat in the booth and fidgeted with the snake shaped ring with the red jewel eyes on her middle finger. Spinning it around and around her finger, sliding it up to the knuckle. She looked at the back of her hand. Didn't like the way the veins showed through. Didn't like a lot of things about her body. Still, some you can fix, some you got to live with. And the stuff she'd got from the doctor was helping things. She had tits to die for already. Marie said it. True enough. Not as sweet a body as Marie but hell, she was much further down the line. It'll come, she thought. Baby, I'm sure spun sugar sweet already but it'll come down easy with Marie at my side.

Marie had hooked up with Jane a couple of months previously,

<24>

back when Jane was called Dolores. Shit, Dolores? What kind of a name is that huh? Dolores is the kind of name you change from not to. Marie had smirked and drawled it out again. Dollorrrrus, ugh. That's really ugly. I'm going to give you another name. I'm going to call you Queen Jane. See it's from Dylan baby. I'm Absolutely Sweet Marie and you're Queen Jane Approximately. You like it?

Jane loved it. Never heard Dylan, at least not that she remembered but she liked it. Absolutely Sweet Marie and Queen Jane Approximately. They stayed together. Marie showed Jane the places to go, where to get clothes that would fit her and how to make some money. She put her in touch with an agent who got her a few club dates early on. Speciality stuff. TV strip shows in grimy back rooms of backstreet pubs around Old Street and the City. A slow grind along to *Lay Lady Lay* or *Rainy Day Women*. Stupid. But the agents loved dumb gimmicks. The punters couldn't give one. If she'd been performing to the speaking clock it'd have been the same deal. The same freakshow and the same guilty hard-ons. Marie had put her on to a doctor who was helping more. Pumping in the hormones. And as Jane's chest started swelling so did her performance fees. She was moving up in class. They still called her a fucking freak and the drunken animals would howl and claw at her as she went through her number but then afterwards they started coming up to her, asking her if she'd like to go somewhere with them. If she'd like to uh, y'know, uh go out for a drink or something. Jane did the something with them whenever she felt like it. Sometimes she would, sometimes she wouldn't. Just do it anytime and every time baby, Marie said. Do it and take the money. It's easy money. Easy. But Jane didn't want to turn into just another blow or boneshake in the back of a taxi. She still had her dream. She still wanted to be in the movies or something. She wanted to be written about and shouted about. Sure thing she wanted to be masturbated over,

<25>

but not while she was in the same room. Man, I don't want the dent I want a fucking crater.

Marie came back from the bar with the drinks and a man followed her and sat down next to them in the booth. Marie introduced them and Jane held out her hand to the man. He kissed it then smiled, flashing his gold tooth.

Marie lit a cigarette. Yeah, Harry said he was feeling a little lonely so I said why don't you come over here and keep my friend company while I go off for a while. Jane glared at Marie who was getting up to leave. You'll be alright here with Harry won't you Jane? She hauled the bag of CDs up from the floor and hung it on her shoulder.

And where are you going?

Marie was standing behind Harry now, she winked and rubbed her fingers together indicating big coin then smiled and said that she was going up to Berwick Street to get rid of the stuff and that she'd just see Jane back at the flat later seeing as how it was barely worth coming back here once she'd gone all the way up into Soho. Marie disappeared out of the door. Jane watched it swing closed and muttered under her breath. Fuck it. She think she's my fucking pimp? Harry said, Huh? Jane smiled and turned to face him. Nothing, sorry. So Harry, what do you do?

Arms spread above him, each wrist cuffed to the radiator, Harry lay naked on the floor.

Piss on me.

What?

I said piss on me.

Queen Jane stepped up onto his chest and dug her six inch heel into his flesh, just below his right nipple. The skin tore and when she moved it away a tiny bubble of blood appeared.

Please. Just do it.

<26>

The Queen moved her foot up to Harry's face and forced the heel into his mouth. Harry started sucking on it and she moved it around, the little metal plate digging into the roof of his mouth scratching the flesh. Harry gagged as she forced the heel in deeper, cutting into his cheek. She was tempted to really kick into him and maybe start chipping at his teeth but she stepped back and stood with her legs apart, either side of his chest. From where she was standing she could see out the window. Two men were leaning out of a window in the office block opposite. Striped shirts and dark ties, smoking cigarettes. An aeroplane flew across the sky. Jane thought about all the people on it, where they were going, what they would be doing when they got there. Harry groaned under her, his chest hitting her heels.

For fuck's sake I'm paying you for this so do it will you!

Jane stepped back a little. The plane had disappeared from sight. She looked down at Harry's expectant face as he wriggled in the cuffs. She lifted her dress and pulled her limp dick out of her panties and held it, the snake ring cool against her flesh. Then she started pissing. Ammonia stink from afternoon alcohol. Yellow. Bright yellow. Harry held his mouth open and she jerked her dick so the stream splashed in his mouth. He wriggled more, moaning, Oh, Oh, Oh. Like a fucking worm, she thought, like a fat pink worm in the rain. When she finished up she shook off the last drops and stepped back, Harry writhed his tongue around, lapping at the piss that ran over his face. Harry's cock flapped. Hard, solid. Touch it, he was screaming, touch the fucking thing. Shit, suck it or something. Pleading now. Please. Now, now, now. Jane raised a foot and dug a spike into his balls. Oh shit, shit, shit. Harry was pumping up and down, back arched. Shit. Oh fuck. Oh. Jane dug her heel in a little more, then Harry burst open on her. Jerking white gunk onto his stomach, the floor. A little on her shoe. She wiped it off against his thigh. Like his cock sneezed or something she thought. And again. More. And Harry's last growl

<27>

and he buried his face in his armpit and his dick twitched empty spasms.

Jane stood at the window and watched the clouds roll by while she waited for Harry to get out of the shower. The room still stank of piss even though the rug Harry had been lying on had been taken up and dumped into a bucket of disinfectant. Fuck. Why did she have to wait around for her money? Couldn't he have paid her before he took the fucking shower? She switched the TV on and began flicking through the cable stations. She watched a video on MTV. Bad metal. Then turned the station again. Harry was singing in the shower. Click. Ice skating. She couldn't make out what he was singing. Click. American TV cops. The shower shut off and Harry kept singing. *On you I will grow...* Click. North By Northwest. *I will grow to hate the like of...* Cary Grant is on the balcony in the bad guy's place on Mount Rushmore. He's trying to get a sign to Eva Marie Saint to tell her not to get on the plane. *What enthralls me so.* Cary Grant throws a book of matches from the balcony. *On arable land I will roam...* Martin Landau walks straight past the matches but he doesn't see them. *To steal from the bed...* Eva Marie Saint finds the matches and looks for Cary Grant. *Of the best friend I've ever known.*

The singing stopped and Jane looked up from the screen as Harry came through the door. He'd changed into a pair of brown chinos and a white teeshirt with a green star across the front. He sat down next to Jane on the sofa. Oh baby that was so good. He put his arm around her shoulder and she shrugged. But not too much. Not until he laid the coin on her. Harry pointed to the screen. You like movies. You ever wanted to be in one? I know people. I could get you in a movie. Sure thing. Yeah. You interested? Yeah, you are? I thought you would be. Yeah, I'll get the number for you. Hold on.

Jane watched the screen. Cary Grant had to stop them getting

<28>

on that plane with all those microfilms. Harry sat back down beside her and gave her a card. Just call this guy. Tell him I gave you the number. Tell him that I recommended you. Jane looked at the card. There was a number printed on it with a code she didn't recognise. Still watching the screen. Say where is this? Harry squeezed her shoulder. Amsterdam. Big studio there. Just call him, tell him Harry sent you. This is for you. Harry pressed a couple of £50 notes into her hand. Thanks. We'll do it again. Call me. Okay.

Jane stood up and straightened her dress. She put the money in her pocket and said goodbye to Harry and thanks a lot. One last look at the TV as she let herself out of the door, then heard Harry start singing again from inside. She'd seen it before. Cary gets the girl. Of course he does.

<29>

Bomb Culture

Harry and Rootboy sat a wooden table breaking up styrofoam cups, tossing the pieces into a pile that was growing like a little fake snow mountain.

Say what did you do to your face?

Huh, my face?

Yeah, you look like you took a punch, your lip's all swollen up.

Harry rubbed his mouth with his open palm, Ah nothing, some guy was itching for something so I took him outside, ha ha, afternoon drunks huh, jus' caught me with his elbow when he was on the way down, y'know. Like as if he was gonna tell the Boy about the Queen and her heels or the way it had been with that gold sprinkling down on him and he thought he was gonna burst, like she'd crushed a toothpaste tube with those six inch spikes and it came out like paste, on and on forever, oh lord help me. So he said: Hey I think we got enough of this stuff now, and crushed a cup in his hand, little white pieces floating to the floor, then threw the husk of it on the pile. He got up and walked over to the metal cabinet in the corner of the room and took out three empty glass bottles and a red plastic five gallon container of gasoline and set them on the table. He motioned to Rootboy to go fetch the wooden box that he'd left in the cabinet, and he lined the bottles up.

Okay get the funnel and fill these bottles with petrol. Just about two thirds full.

Rootboy poured the fluid into the first bottle, slowly, carefully, supporting the weight of the container with his palm. When he had them all filled he capped the container and carried it back to the cabinet.

Harry started dropping the little pieces of polystyrene into the bottles, prodding them down into the petrol with a pencil. He

<30>

swirled a bottle around going, Aaaaaahhhh! Looks just like one of those snowflake things eh? Only thing missing is the plastic Santa Claus. Except I wouldn't want to get a gift like this uh? You?

Rootboy laughed, then frowned: Guess not. Still, if you don't mind me asking what is it with the polystyrene? Couldn't we just throw the fuckers or something?

Finishing up, screwing the cap onto the last bottle, head down, concentrating, Harry looked up thinking, Fucking Christ almighty ain't it obvious, and then smiled patient: No, see petrol just burns up fast, real fast. When we come to use these babies, the polystyrene will have melted into mush in the petrol, this is like homemade napalm, boy. Sticky. So when it goes BOOM, he clapped his hands, it'll spread the flames around, kind of regulate it. Any rate it'll burn long enough to really kick off a fire. Harry laid his palms flat on the table then started tapping his fingers, rapping gold and silver rings on the wood: And we're going to be inside aren't we? You know the Walkway, you've seen it. No windows without grilles, no letterbox to push a thing through. Am I right?

Rootboy nodded.

So it wouldn't be such a great idea to go in there, throw a Molotov and then try to beat the flames back out the door huh? You're getting it, I see you're getting it. Okay, will you just open up the windows in here, these fumes are giving me a fucking headache.

Rootboy opened the windows wide letting in the sound of the traffic rumbling outside. Harry carried the bottles back to the cabinet and stood them on the bottom shelf then closed it up. He walked over to the window and leaned out, taking big gulps of air.

When the fumes had died down he sat back at the table and took out a new pack of nonfiltered Camel cigarettes from his shirt

<31>

pocket. Do you still wear a watch?

Yeah, said Rootboy, showing his wrist, a silver Tag Heuer 6000.

Okay, then get ready to time this. Harry put a cigarette to his lips, struck a match and inhaled. He stood the burning cigarette on its end on the table then leaned back, watching grey smoke plume upwards to be scattered by the breeze from the open window. He got up, careful not to rock the table, and shut it. Laboratory conditions. Harry watched the smoke rising, Rootboy stared at his wrist.

So Harry, what is this we're doing now? Rootboy glanced up from his watch. He was biting his lip, concentrating on that little second timer going around and around.

Harry rocked in his chair, resting on the back legs. He pointed at the upright cigarette: Well the time it takes for one of these cigarettes to burn down to about an inch or so is the amount of time we've got to get clear of the place. What time are we on now?

Rootboy checked the dial and whispered, 2.15, like they were studying the secret life of some wild animal, something that couldn't be startled by any loud noise in case it disappeared out of sight, not like they were both looking at a stick of tobacco burning down.

Okay so we're just over halfway gone, Harry pointed to the glowing tip of the cigarette and the curling grey ash that leaned to the side of it, still attached, So we're probably looking at four minutes, but say three to be safe, which is more than enough.

Harry picked up the cigarette from the table and took a drag then tossed it to the floor and ground it out, spreading blond strands of tobacco across the linoleum. He opened the wooden box and took out a smaller cardboard box, flipped open the lid and held up a little firework, twisting the fuse between his fingertips so that the firework wriggled like a mouse caught by its

<32>

tail. He put another Camel on the table next to the firework then took a red rubber bung and a roll of fuse wire from the box. When he had the things lined out he put his hands together like he was about to pray, then turned them outwards, popping his knuckles.

He grinned: Now pay attention. The ever efficient, and very professional Mr Harold Maynard Fulson is going to demonstrate how to build your very own petrol bomb timer out of, he adopted a condescending voice like he was talking to a child, *everyday household objects*. See we don't need to piss about throwing the things. We place them. Light up the cigarette and when it burns down... Harry paused, Rootboy leaned forward in his chair waiting. Harry's lips tightened, waiting, waiting... BOOOOMM!!! Ha, ha, ha. Harry laughed loud. A second later Rootboy joined him.

<33>

Out In The Open

Warm and hazy night. The last smear of daylight silhouetting buildings across the horizon that bit into the encroaching darkness like decaying teeth. Ray combed back his hair, slick black, still wet from the shower, and pressed his forehead up against the cool glass of the window. All around him lights were flickering on, illuminating cavities in those tall, rotting teeth. He worked a little NuNile pomade into his hair and pulled down a strand so it hung just above his left eye. Looking at his reflection, he curled his lip and growled, one foot planted on the floor the other swivelling on tiptoe, snaking his hips, a vague invocation of a mythical English Presley. Then he laughed at the ineptitude of his impression. Growled an obscenity and turned his back on the reflection.

Ray grabbed the small wad of notes from his pocket and counted it. Just under £100. A week before he'd had a couple of grand. The beginnings of a stake to take him and Lisa clear. The deal had set him up with the opportunity to increase his money by a few hundred per cent. He'd figured on allowing a month to offload then to do the same again, snowballing his money until he had enough. Three maybe four months tops. Rudi had put the brakes on that.

Outside a siren wailed, growing louder as the flashing blue lights lit up the street outside. Ray peered out of the window. As the fire engine sped past he could see the men struggling into their protective yellow overalls. Don't those sirens drive them crazy? Every day another piece of hell on earth. The engine disappeared around the corner and the last trailing wail of the siren faded into the distance.

He pulled the curtain closed and his foot caught the telephone receiver that was still lying face down on the carpet. He picked it

<34>

up and reset it on the cradle.

As his hand touched the door handle on his way out, the phone started to ring. He stared at it for a moment hoping it would stop. It went on ringing.

YEAH?

Ray? Ray Gardner? You may not remember me. I work for Rudi. We, uh, met up after your little indiscretion at the club. This is a message for you from Rudi. He wants to see you. He has a little errand he wants you to run. Come to the club tomorrow. Better say midday. We'll be expecting you.

He recognised the bald man's voice but before he could answer the man had hung up. So, Rudi had called him in. The waiting was over. And now what? He tried to think about what Rudi could want him to do. What would be the worst thing? Whatever happened it was going to be a grade A pain in the arse. Like he had time for this shit. Like he could afford to be hung up on someone else's business.

Wind back. Walking out with his pockets full. Swaggering down the street. Up to Hades. Nod to the doorman. Doing a hundred before even making it up to the bar for the first drink. Thinking about going back to the flat to restock and offload some of the folding. Then... FUCK. He slammed his fist down hard into the sofa sending up a cloud of dust. FUCKIN' WHY? Why had he ever gone to Rudi's club in the first place? It wasn't as though it was difficult to shift elsewhere. He'd been impatient. Rudi's had a rep for high turnover and fast traffic. Rich pickings from rich kids. He might've known Rudi would've had the scene all sewn up. No, he should've known.

The slow, painful buildup then BAM! Gone. He cursed himself for being a fucking idiot. It would take time to get enough money together to start over. He was stuck. He had to stay and play Rudi's game.

He closed his eyes. Every time he closed his eyes he saw her as

<35>

though her image was burned onto his eyelids. Hanging holy. Glorious Titian curls flowing over her shoulders. The way that she'd looked that first time, the night that they'd met. By the time that night had turned to morning they'd decided that they were going to move on together as soon as they could afford it. Ray promised to take care of finding the money. They didn't know where they were heading but somewhere. Somewhere else. Only when they'd decided this did they go to bed and fuck while the city rubbed the sleep from its eyes.

The night air felt cool on his still damp hair. Hands deep in pockets, Ray gazed up at the sky, running from pink to deep, dark blue the higher he looked. He kicked a can as he walked along and whistled the hook to a top forty song that he'd been trying to shake out of his head all day. He glanced at his watch. If he took a cab instead of the tube he'd have time to get a couple of drinks before he was due to meet Lisa. A change of scene. More time to think. More time to be running blank, back out in the open.

He turned into a side street as a short cut. On either side were vast metal warehouses and factories. Bright red or blue by day, by night the sick yellow street lamps drank their colour casting them in shades of grey. The howl of the machines, the sound of metal clanging. Whirring forklifts darted in and out of gaping doorways, shifting pallets piled high, trailing plastic wrap, into waiting, headless artics.

Ahead he heard a scream. He looked up and saw a young boy hurtling towards him on a skateboard, swinging a blue leather bag in his hand. As the boy drew level, Ray thrust out his arm, catching him on the side of the head and sending him to the floor. The board careered on down the street until it hit the kerb and skidded along on its back, wheels spinning in the air like an upturned beetle's desperate legs. Ray yanked the boy to his feet,

<36>

squeezing his arm, his fingernails digging into the youthful soft skin.

I think you have something that doesn't belong to you. He pointed to the handbag the boy was still clutching. The boy stared at Ray with the arrogance of ignorance.

Fuck you, mister. This is my mother's. He waved the bag with his free hand. I'm just going shopping for her. The boy grinned.

Ray laughed and called him a stupid fuck then prised the bag out of the boy's grip, opening the clasp with one hand. Barked at him, Okay you little shit. I'll give you a chance. What's your mother's name? He gripped the boy's arm tighter and shook him a little when he didn't answer. Still silence and Ray squeezed harder until his fingernails pierced the boy's skin, making tiny, arced incisions on his upper arm. Well kid, you don't know your mother's name. Huh?

The boy began to squeal and kick out. Ray let go of his arm dropping him to the floor. Instantly he was up and lunging forward. He threw a punch towards Ray's head but it was blocked easily and he was knocked off balance. Ray aimed the point of his boot at the boy's stomach and as he fell forward, Ray brought his knee up into the boy's face. He crumpled to the floor, blood streaming from a broken nose. He got up spitting and swinging. Tried for a right hook. Ray ducked. Went for a left jab. Ray blocked then grabbed his arm, bending it back against the elbow.

This'll break. Another little push. I tell you this'll break.

Ray kicked the kid hard in the stomach and let him fall to the floor gasping. Then he hauled him to his feet and whispered that it would be a good idea if he was to get his board and go now before it became necessary to do any lasting harm. It would save them both a lot of trouble. The boy swayed a little and staggered off down the street holding his nose, vainly trying to staunch the flow of blood.

<37>

Ray picked up the handbag and stuffed it under his jacket. He ducked into an alleyway that ran between two of the factory buildings. Leaning in the shadows, his back against the metal railings, Ray took the bag from his jacket and shook the contents out onto the dirt. From a large, fake snakeskin purse he pulled out some cards. Amex, Visa, a cheque card. Mrs Elizabeth Tempest, thankyou very much. He took the few notes from the purse and pocketed them with the cards. Poking amongst the screwed up tissues and sweet wrappers that lay on the ground, Ray found the chequebook and a gold cigarette lighter. He tried the lighter twice and when it failed to spark he tossed it over his shoulder, wincing as it clanged against the railings. Ray put the chequebook with the rest of the stuff and casually walked out of the alley and continued up the street.

<38>

The Baddest Man On The Planet

The King Solomon looked like it had been closed down for years. It stood on its own on a patch of wasteland, the buildings that once kept it company having been demolished. Inside, the the place was quiet, just the click of pool balls from the back room and the subdued talk of a couple of flame-faced men hunched over newspapers at the far end of the counter.

Surrounded by half-built office blocks, the place didn't pull much passing trade. The pub was used at lunchtime by workers on at least three construction sites in the surrounding area, which was gradually being torn down and rebuilt. In the afternoon the Solomon was heaving, by early evening it was empty and stayed that way pretty much the whole night. The landlord was biding his time. He didn't care that there were no customers, it meant less work for him, but he looked after those he had by turning a blind eye and a deaf ear as required in exchange for the odd consumer durable at a special rate, that or a free case of spirits.

In the mirror behind the bar, Ray could see Harry and Rootboy in their usual spot, sucking on bottles of imported beer. Rootboy roared with laughter, an annoying habit of his. Harry, at least, wasn't that funny. Ray knew that. But when they were together Rootboy was always laughing. And they were always together. The barman was staring up at a TV showing a troupe of girls doing some synchronised hula-hooping. A talent show or something, Ray guessed. He caught the barman's eye and ordered a drink. As he poured the drink, the barman gestured to the screen, Bet they fuck like crazy huh? He rolled his hips. Ray nodded blankly.

Pinned up above the bar and running right along its length were dozens of bad cheques, displayed like other pubs have foreign bank notes. There was a crudely inked sign, stark white

<39>

against the grimy, red flock paper. ABSOLUTELY NO CHEQUES CASHED. The barman brought over the drink then continued staring at the screen, his tongue flicking in and out of his mouth and across his lips like a reptile's. Ray took his drink and walked over to Harry and Rootboy.

Raaay, Harry drawled, flashing a glimpse of gold tooth and pushing out a chair with the heel of his black, patent leather shoe. So good to see you. What brings you here? He clicked his tongue, smiled. And man, aren't you looking like something?

Ray shook Rootboy's extended hand and sat down between the two men.

I had some time to kill and I thought I'd find you here. Ray tapped at his pocket. I've got a couple of items you could clear for me.

Rootboy leaned back on his chair, balancing with his feet curled around the leg of the table. He rolled his beer bottle between his hands so the glass caught against the rings on his fingers and it sounded like an engine starting up.

A long, thin scar curved from his temple to the corner of his mouth, then straight down, but thicker, to his chin, so he looked like a badly made ventriloquist's dummy. One time at a fast food place he had gone to take a piss after ordering his food. While he was at the urinal and, as he always made sure to point out, in mid flow with his hands on his dick, somebody had come up from behind and lifted his wallet from his hip pocket. When he turned to face the thief, he felt something brush across his face and the next thing he knew, he was standing there with his cheek flapping from a razor slash, blood pouring down his shirt and piss pouring over his trousers.

Yeah, Ray. So what you got?

Ray took a sip from his drink and leaned forward, speaking in a whisper. Fresh cards, not an hour old. Visa, Amex, chequebook, all female.

<40>

Rootboy laughed, loud, cackling, causing the old men at the bar to look over at the table. Whaaaat? Ray, I thought you were above all this. Times so hard that you're hustling old ladies for their purses? You'll be back on the creeps like a fuckin' teenager next. Rootboy, laughing so much he was shaking, reset his chair squarely on the floor and took a noisy slurp from his bottle and pointed at Ray. Hear him H, fuckin' cards man, fuckin' cards and we thought he'd moved on up.

Ray lit a cigarette and cursed under his breath. Rootboy taking the piss was a little much to bear.

Harry looked at Ray and then over at Rootboy who was still giggling. He motioned for him to cut it out then leaned towards Ray and spoke. Sure, we'll take them. We'll give you £50 for the set. He caught Ray's frown then came back with, Come on Ray, we don't do this kind of thing much anymore. I'm prepared to take them off your hands but it's only because I'm doing you a favour. You can owe me one.

Ray banged his glass down hard, slopping out a little beer onto the table top. Some favour. The going rate was £50 per card, more for a good credit card like the Amex. At least it was the last time he'd been in this position and he doubted that the price had dropped. This had been a stupid idea all round. Stupid to take the cards in the first place and even more stupid to try to sell them on. Especially to these two. Whatever he got for them would hardly make it worth all the hassle. Still, money was money and he needed it. He'd come all the way out here to find them.

Hey look, if you say £50 it's £50. Just don't give me any of that 'favour' shit. Take them.

He threw a look over to the barman who was still gazing up at the TV, then handed the cards and book over. Harry peeled a note off a thick, pink wad, gave it to Ray and then passed another to Rootboy and told him to fetch some more drinks. He ambled over to the bar. Harry and Ray sat and talked.

<41>

Rootboy set a tray on the table and slid back into his chair. He nodded to Ray and pointed at the bottles. Take one... You still running with the same girl huh? What's her name now? Rootboy stared into space. Ray could see his brain rolling like a buckled wheel under his wrinkled forehead. Ray reached for a bottle, thinking Christ no, not the small talk. And then, after an age, Lisa, yeah, you still with that Lisa?

Yeah, I'm still with Lisa. Are you still living with your mother?

Harry smirked as Rootboy nodded, embarrassed, and then he turned to Ray. Well, we heard you had a little trouble with Rudi. Is that right? You better stay clean with him. We heard he got the Walkway closed down. Burned the shithouse down. Doused the place in petrol then doused the manager and, uh, lit the blue touchpaper and stood well back. When the poor guy went running through to get out onto the street the insides caught and BOOM! Harry clapped his hands. The whole fuckin' lot just tore up.

Ray smiled uncomfortably. Rootboy began to laugh uncontrollably, muttering, Fantastic. It was fuckin' fantastic. Harry pulled a cigarette from a crumpled box of Camel and then offered the pack around. Ray took one and Rootboy lit it with an expensive looking tortoiseshell lighter then, through a cloud of smoke: Have you heard my man's latest? This one's a peach.

Ever since Ray had known him, Harry had been the master of the crackpot scheme. Almost always involving a way to get very rich, very quick and almost always verging on the ridiculous. Ray could see by the way that Harry leaned forwards ready to give him the spiel that this was another lame horse hobbling out of Harry's ideas stable. As he always pointed out, if Harry was so hot and his mind was such a goldmine (a favourite phrase he just knew he was going to hear in the next thirty seconds) then why was he always hustling smalltime and why was he always sitting in a bar with Rootboy, desperately looking for someone else to

<42>

talk to?

In a final attempt to put off the inevitable Ray pointed this out to Harry again, leaving out the bit about the Boy so as not to hurt his feelings.

Harry shrugged his shoulders. Ray looked at the ceiling. It hadn't worked.

Why are you always trying to put me down hey? So I don't get the luck. Had the breaks I could be living like a king. I'm an ideas man. You know it. By rights I should have me a plush office with a couple of nice girls attending to me. My mind is gold man, fucking eighty four carat and people ought to pay me every time I roll a little off for them.

Ray winced when he heard the reference to gold. This must be one of his more outlandish schemes seeing as how he'd upped himself sixty carats since the last time. Ray leaned back and listened.

This is the best yet. And keep it to yourself too, okay. Don't say a word until I've been in touch with the right people. I throw these things out like I'm throwing loose change at beggars and they get stolen every time and every fucker gets rich off them but me. This, he tapped his head, is a Midas machine.

After this build-up Ray feared the worst. He was hoping that he wouldn't laugh in Harry's face. I'm listening. Looking at the ceiling. The TV set. The wallpaper. The bottom of his glass. I'm listening.

Okay. So I came up with this one just this morning. I'm gonna sell it to that boxing guy with the electric hair. This is the big one for that boy of his. See, no one can beat him. NO FUCKING ONE can get near him when he's on for it. And when he's down man, he's the baddest man on this planet. They're all gonna be crying no mas! and mewling like puppies in a dunking sack. They're all lining up and he's just knocking 'em down. This is all getting to be pretty boring right? Am I right? So, what he does is

<43>

he hires himself a big jet, like a fuckin' 747 or something and he builds a ring inside the plane. Yeah, I can see you're getting it. So he flies the fuckin' world picking up the champion out of each continent and dumping them on their backsides as he flies on to the next place. Could even take on one of those Sumo fuckers and pull in some Yen. Japs would go for it. And the Japs will bet on anything, like how many legs does that fly have?

Harry jabbed his finger at a fly that had started crawling along the rim of an empty glass on the table. Yeah. Six. You say six. I say six. The Boy here will say six. But I could get a Jap to lay out on five. Give him good odds and he'd go four or seven. I've seen it. Anyway we sell the TV rights but the thing is, only the real, fuckin' ultra, eeeeemaculate rich are going to be able to afford ringside. It'll be your Sinatras, your film stars... Stallone maybe, this sure beats the crap out of any of those Rocky films hey? It'll be the kick of the century. The ultimate mile high club. And when it happens, I'm going to be there. It's worth millions and you're laughing. I tell you when you're an old man skinning up pipe tobacco and sipping on ruby wine I'm gonna have a mansion and girls washing my feet with their hair. It only takes one thing to come through, just one hit, I've got it all ahead of me. My mind is an ideas machine gun.

Ray stopped laughing and drained his bottle. To be honest, this was one of Harry's better ideas. The funniest thing was the way that Rootboy had been slapping his thighs, urging Harry on like he was riding in a Derby winner. Ray took an elaborate look at his watch and thanked the men for the beer. He told them that he had an appointment, that he had to go though of course he'd love to stay and talk all night and, sure, sure he'd see them again soon. He left them sucking on their beers and contemplating Harry's riches ahead as he walked back out into the night air barely hiding his smile.

He walked towards the tube station, keeping his eyes open for

<44>

any cabs on the road. At the entrance of the tube a man was dancing in a circle on the pavement, swinging a broken umbrella around his head. A windmill blur of chromed metal and black nylon. When Ray got closer he could see loose change scattered over a plastic shopping bag on the floor and he could hear that the man was singing. The words were there but the tune had been left at the bottom of some bottle. The lights of the underground station back lit the dancer as he revolved under the awning. It was as close to a stage as he was ever going to get.

Behind him a couple of men were slumped in an alcove, their dark clothes blending in with the soot and grime like they were two oily rags thrown into the corner of a garage. The men swigged on a bottle and, seeing Ray, chorused: Aaaah give the fucken singer some, eh sir? Give the man some.

Ray reached into his pocket and pulled out one of the notes he'd taken from the purse. He screwed it up into a ball in the palm of his hand and flicked it towards the carrier bag with his thumbnail. Before it hit the pavement, the breeze caught it and it blew along the ground and nestled amongst a pile of food wrappers and crushed paper cups that had gathered around the feet of a broken concrete bench. The man danced on. He hadn't noticed. The blue-green queen's head stared up from the rubbish, crumpled into a mocking wink.

A taxi cab moved along the street and Ray raised his hand. He climbed inside, gave the driver his destination and sank back into the tartan covered seat as the driver eased the vehicle back into the flow of traffic. The cab began to worm its way into the belly of the city. From the rear window Ray watched the man whirl the umbrella around his head, the black nylon flapping noisily as though it were the broken wings of a giant steel and fabric bird desperately struggling to fly away.

<45>

Any Kind Of Star

Jane sat on the unmade bed, a Polaroid camera in her lap, opening it up, tearing open a new carton of film, sliding it in. Her head resting against the wall. A creased poster of Dylan in a cap with an acoustic guitar. Sprayed behind her in 18 inch letters, gold paint, simple block capitals. FUCK FOREVER. The fuck starting just by Dylan's ear. She held the camera up to her face. Pointed it over at Marie, sitting in the armchair, magazine open, glass of gin and tonic. Flash. The photograph faded in from grey. Image sharpening like an old TV set humming on. Red lips. Smile coming clearer. She called over to Marie who laid the magazine on the arm of the chair.

So are you going to come too?

I don't know, I guess maybe. What exactly did he say?

He said that I should come over and that he'd have a great part for me and if I knew anybody else that I should bring them along too.

And did he say what kind of part it was? What sort of film is it?

No he didn't but I can guess.

Yeah, so can I. And my guess is that it's not going to be the kind of film that wins any awards.

So what. Of course it's going to be a porno. But hell, that's still a film isn't it? I don't see anyone else offering us the chance to make a movie.

Baby, I could make a call right now and get you a part in a porn film and you wouldn't even need to leave the borough to do it.

Yeah, okay. But they wouldn't be offering me expenses over a travelcard or a three digit fee.

So what did the guy in Amsterdam offer?

Well we'd have to pay for the flight and accommodation but

<46>

he's guaranteed my name on the opening credits and my picture on the front of the video box. Plus three Gs up front and two points on the net profit and, and this is most important, he said he was going to make me a star.

Yeah, a porn star!

Shit, so what. Any kind of star is still a star. And any kind of star is more than I am now.

Jane jumped up from the bed and walked over to Marie and kissed her on the forehead. The copy of Obituary Monthly magazine that she'd been looking at had a cover story about the unexplained shooting of a supermodel. Headline: Looks Can Kill – *Morton Fisher Reporting.* Marie looked up. Jane smiled, and then whispered in her ear, Oh please come, please, it'll be fun, really, please. She flashed the Polaroid photograph in front of Marie's face. See how good you look on film. Wow. Look.

Marie got out of the chair and walked over to the wardrobe. She started sifting through the clothes on the hangers. Then she turned and sighed, Okay baby you got me, how long have we got? When are we going because I've gotta pack.

<47>

Nowhere Fast

Taxi pulls up in a dim lit side street. Cheap yellow and red plastic sign. Blackboard on the brickwork. Faded menu. Smudged pastel chalk strokes merge like the pattern of a butterfly's wings. People stumble out the door, glasses in hand. Ray pushes past, down marble steps, worn at the edges, worn smooth. Holding onto the rail as three more men pass, snatches of their conversation. Yeah, you've got to see it. I tell you. I'm going for it. Really. Yeah, I'll show you. Frame by frame. Well what a bitch. She wouldn't have done that for me VCR or no VCR. You're the fucking devil hisself, Steward, the fucking devil. Sold your soul for a ten year boner. And don't I know what to do with it. Laugh. A hiss like a spike being pulled from a car tyre. Yessssssssssssssss.

Lisa had been waiting for Ray in the cellar bar for the past twenty-five minutes. In that time she'd smoked a couple of cigarettes and drunk two glasses of Powers with coke. She was crunching on an icecube from the bottom of her glass and thinking about calling Ray to see if he'd even left yet but decided against it, seeing as how she'd only lose her seat at the bar and would then have to jostle for a space to stand in the cramped room. A version of *Volare* came onto the jukebox and a group of drunks in a corner booth started up with the chorus chanting *Woahohohoh!* She looked at the wall clock again and leaned over the bar, rattling the icecubes in her glass.

Ray saw her as soon as he reached the bottom of the steps. He moved through the crowd until he came up behind her. Put his arms around her. When she turned to face him she was wearing a huge grin and Ray thought that he'd never seen anyone as pleased to see someone. She made him feel like a pair of wings were

<48>

sprouting out of his back. All holy. Beatific. He kissed her softly on the lips. And he sure as hell couldn't remember ever being as pleased to see somebody as he was at that moment. Ray ordered two more from a stick slim Spaniard with a wart on the end of his nose like a budding rhino horn.

The drunken chorus of *Volare* staggered Dean Martin style out of their booth and Ray guided Lisa over to the free table. He pushed all the used glasses to the side and sat opposite Lisa reaching over, holding her hand. Watching her lips move. A silent movie. Then he heard her talking and then the fade up of garbled conversation and glasses clattering and the room was full again like the pause button had been released.

...Yeah I did it Ray. Ha, it was so cool. So funny.

Did what?

It was as easy as you'd said it would be. I didn't even need to come on to him...

Ray picked up on what she was telling him. He smiled at Lisa. You know I didn't think you'd really do it. I only said it as a joke. Are you sure he's not going to make a complaint?

Who to? Anyway, the girl you told me about. No one complained about her did they?

Oh yeah right. That girl. The thing about it is. See there wasn't any girl. I only said it as a joke. I made it up.

You what? Lisa laughed. Oh, I guess it doesn't really matter anyway. I only got about £300. I was going to wait until we'd had a really busy day, but today... Her voice trailed off as she tried to find words to explain just how mad she'd been. ...And it was so exciting. I didn't mean to throw the bottle but I had it there in my hand and I just wanted to see it smash. I just felt that I had to throw it.

Then Ray laughed and squeezed Lisa's hand a little harder. Reached up and brushed a strand of hair from her face. Just don't make a habit of it hey?

<49>

Me? What about you? So are you going to tell me what's going on? Or have I got to carry on dreaming up all kinds of reasons a man might have for telling a woman that he can't see her for a few days. That she can't even call him. I only called today because the yarns I was spinning myself were getting so tangled I was scared they'd end up strangling me. So are you going to tell me now or have you turned into some kind of mystery man? No. No. Don't tell me. You're working for the government. It's a spy deal right? Or are you working for the other side? No. I got it. I know now. You've been podded and you're preparing the earth for invasion from outer space. That's it, huh? Come on Ray. My bullshit detector's on standby.

Ring Of Fire started up on the jukebox and while Johnny Cash went down, down, down Ray laid out the situation to date. By the end of the number Lisa was shaking her head and Ray was assuring her that it only sounded bad.

It won't take long, I promise you baby. Leaning across the table for a kiss. No time at all. So, that's how it is. I'll see him tomorrow and then...

Why don't we just go? Tonight.

But I've just told you. He's cleaned me out. We don't even have a grand between us. We couldn't get anywhere worth going with the money we've got and, even if we could, we'd be no better off when we got there. So, for now we'll sit tight. And I don't want to even think about it until tomorrow.

Ray picked up their empty glasses and motioned towards the bar.

What are we going to do then?

Well I guess we could have some more here and then go on somewhere else. A club. Or something. Whatever you want. You're the one that just got out of the cage.

<50>

The club was called Hypnomonotony and it was housed in a converted railway arch way out in the east of the city. When they arrived, it was already heaving. Music pumped relentlessly from speakers that seemed to be situated in every corner Ray looked. Footage of rockets, missiles, plane crashes, riots and wars fast cut with loops from black and white stag films flashed across the whitewashed brick walls from a battery of projectors set high up in the corner. The curve of the ceiling caused the faces of 50's glamour queens to stretch and distort as they unhooked their corsets and rolled down their stockings, over and over again. Beneath scenes of sex and blood and death, the crowd danced on.

Lisa moved towards the bar. Ray noticed a small stage, raised on blocks, about four feet off the floor. A banner hung over the back of it with the word UNLISTENABLE scrawled across it in paint that caught the UV light so the letters glowed as if they were burning in an alcohol fire. He looked around at all the people dancing, then moved quickly to catch up with Lisa, who was disappearing into the mess of people around the bar. Ray jostled through a crowd of sweating, bare-chested boys who were moving to a rhythm Ray was damned if he could hear. He caught up with Lisa and pulled her out of the throng. Shouting, Let me get these. Pointing at the floor. Exaggerated sign language: wait for me here.

He shoulder-charged his way through a gap that had briefly opened up, spilling most of some man's drink over the crotch of a tall blond gym queen in a muscle vest and lycra shorts. This was fucking madness. A snake pit. The music died down for a second and was replaced by something with the exact same tone. The sound pulsated, bass heavy, and Ray was feeling the vibrations through his whole body. He held a twenty aloft and waved it in the general direction of the bar, still some feet away. Let me get a fucking drink for Christ sake. The people immediately in front of Ray parted slightly to allow a girl, balancing three drinks between

<51>

her clasped hands, to move out. Ray saw the gap and went for it, knocking the drinks and the girl to the ground. She was swallowed up by the crowd as they converged on the bar again and no one could have heard the girl's protests even if they had cared enough to listen.

When Ray was finally served he ordered a triple for Lisa, two bottles of beer, and a straight double vodka and ice. He paid the girl and downed the vodka in one before even attempting to move from the bar. Once he was back with Lisa he could feel his shirt and jacket sticking to his body with sweat. He ushered her towards a corner where there was a little more room.

What the fuck is this? He gestured around him with the bottle.

I said we didn't have to come. I knew you wouldn't like it, Lisa shouted in Ray's ear.

But what is it? He had to repeat the question three times before she made out what he was saying. Louder still. It's not even proper music. God knows what all these people are dancing to. Whatever they're on, you gotta get me some. I could clean up.

Ray gave up trying to be heard over the sounds and they just stood watching the people pass in front of them. Lisa caught sight of an old friend of hers and shouted to Ray that she was going to follow her and bring her over to meet him. He watched her disappear, sucked into the mass of bodies.

Ray leaned against the wall and scanned the crowd. He caught sight of a couple of small time dealers that he'd run into in the past. As far as he was aware they were independent operators which meant that the club was free, for the moment at least. If he could stand it he might have to return here. It was certainly busy. He watched, amused, as they mingled with the crowd, hustling the dancers. Hands clenched like cheap magicians and the surreptitious movements that were just so obvious.

There was some action on the stage and the sound from the speakers was replaced by feedback as the guitar amplifiers came

<52>

on. The room fell into darkness. Ray felt a tap on his shoulder and turned to see Lisa by his side. She was with a small, dark woman with a black crew cut. The woman said hello and Lisa handed Ray another bottle.

This is Mona, she used to live in a cave in Spain.

Ray wondered whether that was any way to introduce somebody but he held out his hand and they shook.

What was it like?

Mona looked blankly at him. He repeated the question, mumbling, trying to light a cigarette at the same time.

She's deaf Ray. She lip-reads. You'll have to take the cigarette out of your mouth.

Ray removed the cigarette. To be honest he wasn't really interested what it was like living in a cave. He could imagine. He remembered Lisa telling him all about it anyway. He never understood these back-to-nature types. It seemed dumb as hell to him. He asked again and nodded as Mona told him about her cave.

They seemed to be having some trouble getting the microphones to work and a man was busy counting up to three over and over as his voice cut in and out. Ray was nodding as Mona continued, not really listening but adding an oh really and right right whenever it seemed appropriate. Before he'd even noticed that she'd finished speaking, Mona was giving Lisa a peck on the cheek and then a wave to him as she walked away.

That was really rude. You could have at least pretended that you were interested.

Uh, oh yeah. I suppose so. It's just that you already told me all about it once. Ray shrugged his shoulders. Anyway, while she was talking I was wondering why she was here. Why would a deaf person go to a nightclub?

Because she enjoys it. Simple as that. She's probably enjoying it more than you are anyway.

<53>

It's not that I'm not enjoying myself. It's just that I don't really understand it. The music isn't music, is it? It's just noise.

But that's the concept Ray. It's Hypnomonotony. She gave a wry grin. The point is that the sounds they play here are ones we hear every day. Except here we're supposed to listen to them differently. Detuned radio signals, fax machine tones, engine noises, static, feedback, whatever. The DJs just grab all these sounds and layer them on top of each other. You pick up on whatever rhythms you want from the sound. The idea is that because there really isn't a beat or anything you can consciously latch onto then you can dance as fast or as slow as you like. The sound changes to fit your mood. It's supposed to be therapeutic.

Lisa. That is the biggest pile of bullshit I think I've ever heard.

Yeah isn't it? I read about it in a magazine.

One of the projectors started rolling again, casting a blurred image over four figures who had walked onto the stage. The picture was pulled into focus as the band started up on the first number. Another stag loop, this time in colour and of a more recent vintage. A closeup of an erect cock, a twenty-second loop that ended in ejaculation. The money shot. As the music built up, the drummer started pounding on his cymbal. Every time he hit it, the gunk flowed. Another projector started throwing images at the band, footage of a space shuttle. The image placed so that the shuttle exploded over and over as it reached the tip of the cock. The flames then mixed with the semen. Two guitars opened up spraying feedback over the room. People were jamming their fingers in their ears. It was hard to tell where the noise was coming from exactly. It seemed to spread and fill every space in the club as if it were some heavy liquid.

Suddenly the sound stopped dead and the pictures cut out. One of the band walked up to the microphone. He spoke softly. Hello, we're The Nowhere Fast. Hope you'll all endure this. We make a noise. What more can we do? This is called *Impact Zone.*

<54>

The room was in darkness. Total silence for a split second. The singer let out a scream and four huge strobes came on at the back of the stage pointing straight out into the audience. The drummer started beating out a basic 4/4 beat and the guitars cut in with slabs of squealing feedback. The singer was yelping, throwing himself around the stage and running the mic stand up and down the lead guitarist's fretboard like a slide. One hell of a racket.

The singer was wearing a white tuxedo with black, baggy trousers. His hair was swept up into a faintly ridiculous conical quiff and he wore long sideburns and a pencil moustache. When the song ended, most of the crowd whooped and applauded. The others, who were covering their eyes from the constant assault of the strobe lights, looked at the floor or moved towards the bar mumbling.

From behind a curtain another band member ambled on and sat himself behind an electric piano that was raised above the stage on a low platform to the left of the drumkit. The singer pointed at him and he ran his fingers along the keys, starting up another song. When it came to the break, the piano player went crazy, pounding out a solo with his fists, feet, elbows and forehead, attacking the ivories like he was killing elephants. The song ended with the drummer standing up and walking straight through his kit, scattering drums and cymbals across the stage. The singer and guitarists watched him walk off, looked at each other and then followed. The pianist stood, bowed, and then pulled at the banner on the wall, pulled it down, wrapped himself in it and departed, hands punching the air like a victorious heavyweight champ. The strobes were switched off and the crowd were left calling to an empty stage. The band had been playing for less than ten minutes.

Ray drained his bottle and tossed it to the floor. The DJ started up again and the vibrations of an amplified pneumatic drill began to shake up his insides. He put his arm around Lisa and asked her

<55>

if she wanted to stay for a while or go on somewhere else. Lisa kissed him and said that she wanted him to take her home.

<56>

1000 Eyes

The cab pulled up outside Lisa's with a jolt that threw Ray forward as he was trying to make the fare from his jacket pocket. He leaned through the gap in the seats to pay the driver. He'd been staring at the back of the driver's head all the way back. Saw the grey hair and the little specks of dandruff on the back of the seat as the cab moved under bright street lights. He'd seen the back of his head alright, but when he turned around with his hand out... Christ! he looked like an albino Esquerita, stacked silver hair, all that was missing was the diamante spangling on his spectacles. He thanked the driver, told him to keep the change and banged his head on the car door as he stepped out backwards, still staring. The driver stared back, then slipped the car into gear and pulled away.

Hey, baby. Did you see that guy? The driver? Who'd he remind you of?

Lisa was rummaging in her bag for her keys, moving towards the front door.

Quiet Ray, you'll wake her.

Did you see him though?

Who?

The driver.

Yeah, what about him?

What about him? What about him? It was fucking ESQUEEEERRRITTA!!! he screamed, waving his arms in the direction that the cab had gone.

Lisa grabbed him and put her hands over his mouth trying to gag the noise he was making.

Keep it down Ray for God's sake. You're drunk and I don't know what you're talking about.

Esquerita. You know. He taught Little Richard everything he

<57>

knew. He was this wild fag rocker from the 50s. The wildest. Ray let out some Little Richard style hollers and hammered away again on an imaginary piano then tried to sing some more through Lisa's fingers that were again clamped over his mouth.

He broke away from her and started acting out a piano break on the privet hedge at the bottom of the garden, *Aaahm just battie over Hattie Wooooh! Hattie's just battie over me WOOOOOH!* He was hopping on one leg, running his other heel over the green and yellow leaves when he slipped and landed on his back, laughing.

Lisa hauled him to his feet. He opened his mouth and started to sing again, quietly now, smiling, teasing her. She slapped her palm over his mouth again and led him towards the door.

I told you we had to be quiet. I'm not supposed to have visitors stay over. It's in the contract.

Okay, sorry. I'll keep it shut. I don't know why we didn't go back to my place.

Because mine was nearer but it's probably too late now anyway. She's going to be listening at the door to see if I bring you inside.

She opened the door and they walked into the hallway and Ray opened his mouth wide and shaped a long *Woooooh!* but this time it came out silent. When he saw the look on Lisa's face he was laughing again, biting the back of his hand to stop himself and Lisa was laughing with him, resigned.

Ray turned his back to Lisa and gestured for her to get on. One set of footsteps only, he whispered.

He climbed the stairs carefully, footsteps heavy as he tried to keep Lisa balanced on his back. She leaned into his neck and kissed his ear. Ray turned his head slightly towards her and whispered, Well there might only be one set of footsteps but anybody'll wonder how you got to weigh twenty stone and walk like an elephant on the creep.

<58>

By the time they reached the door to her room, up three flights of narrow stairs, Lisa's head was buried in Ray's shoulder, biting mouthfuls of his jacket, trying to stifle her laughing. She jumped off and fumbled with the key at the door as Ray kissed her neck. The door open, she pulled Ray into the room and dragged him over towards the bed. In the darkness Ray reached out behind him for something solid, Lisa pulling off his jacket and pushing him backwards until he fell onto the cool cotton sheets.

Lie down Ray for Christ sake.

Ray was on his back on the bed, his feet still touching the floor. He rubbed the darkness into his eyes, the curtains were back lit grey by the street lights. Lisa's hair shone in the half light as she was on her knees working on his belt, hands running over his legs, pulling on his zipper. When she had the belt loose, she pulled down his trousers, he arched his back a little so that she could remove his shorts. Ray ran his hand through her hair as she kissed his cock, hands stroking and cradling his balls. She bit a little flesh on his thigh then started sucking and he moaned and looked up towards the ceiling and grabbed a fistful of her hair, letting it slip between his fingers. Lisa hauled herself up onto the bed and climbed on top of Ray. Hiking up her dress, she eased his cock inside her.

Fuck me.

She rocked slowly backwards and forwards, bending down to kiss Ray as he ran his hands across her back. Lisa unbuttoned her dress and pulled it over her head and Ray reached up into the darkness. His hands found her breasts and he arched his back, raising himself up so that he could catch a nipple between his lips, his nails raking gently along the curve of her spine. Sure, yet soft enough not to mark the skin.

It's too dark Ray. I need to see you.

Lisa reached for the lamp on the bedside cabinet. Ray rested his forearm over his eyes in anticipation of the light. After a few

<59>

seconds he thought his eyes could take the glare and he uncovered them. Lisa was moving faster on him, one hand propped on the mattress beside him, keeping her balance while the other was behind her back stroking his balls. Ray stared up at the ceiling. Stuck around the light fitting were hundreds and hundreds of pairs of eyes, cut from magazines, newspapers, colour and black and white, spreading out across the ceiling like an incredible fungus. All the eyes were staring straight at him. He felt his dick going limp inside Lisa. He stopped moving and stared up at the eyes. They stared right back.

What's the matter?

Uh, nothing baby. I, uh, I, do you think we could try it the other way?

Lisa rolled off him and onto her back, Ray climbed on and started again. He could still feel the eyes bearing down on his back but for now he could ignore them. Tomorrow he'd ask Lisa when and why she'd put them there. Shit it was a freak. He kept at it, all the time feeling like he was putting on some kind of live bed show.

<60>

Class Acts

Rootboy's hips hammered against the machine and he slammed his fist down hard onto the glass top. TILT flashed up on the dot matrix display and the ball trickled between the two, useless flippers. He cursed the thing then dug around in his pocket looking for another coin. Magnets! This table is fucking fixed. There's fucking magnets under there. He turned to where Harry and the man were sitting. Do either of you have any change, huh? I'm gonna beat this fucking thing yet.

Harry shrugged his shoulders and Rootboy kicked the pinball machine then walked over to Gianni at the counter and asked him for another coffee and said to make sure he made the change for the table.

Forgive my friend, he's a little, uh, impatient. Easily annoyed.

Harry was speaking to a thin man who was nervously fingering the menu and sliding some black framed spectacles up and down his nose. He had been sitting at the table for the past half hour and Harry still hadn't given him the chance to explain what he'd come to talk about. Every time the thin man started to speak, Harry would interrupt and read out a story from the morning paper about some film star who was getting a divorce or a boy who was stuck in a hole, then carry on eating the greasy breakfast he had in front of him. The thin man was tired. He hadn't slept for 48 hours and he was getting impatient. There had to be somebody else who could help him out. He just didn't know anybody else. This was the first time for him. He didn't know this guy. He didn't know anything about him. He wasn't even a friend of a friend. He'd been recommended as the man who, for a price, would know how to help him out. But he was beginning to wonder. He drained the last mouthful from his coffee. He couldn't remember how many he'd drunk already, but the caffeine was

<61>

making him more edgy. He was shook and just about ready to call the whole thing off.

Harry folded up the newspaper and laid it down over his ketchup stained plate. He stared at the man.

So, I'm told you have a problem. Would you like to explain it to me?

The man glanced around him. A couple of men in bus company uniforms were sitting at the table opposite filling out a crossword. At the counter an old man was chewing on a sandwich. Steam rose from the coffee machine and the owner had his back turned and was busy frying food.

Well, you see it's like this. The Welshman gave me your name. He told me I could find you here in the mornings. My name is...

Harry raised his hand.

Look. You don't know my name and I don't need to know your name. In fact I don't want to know your name. Just carry on.

Right, uh, okay. See I did a job. A good one, clean. No problems except that well, I'm kind of stuck. The end product is uh, causing me a few headaches.

What sort of job? Harry was picking bits of bacon from between his teeth.

A supermarket. No, it's okay. Not local. Up north.

You did this on your own?

No, me and one other guy.

And...?

Well it's like this. We thought that we'd hit it and get away with straight bags of cash but what we got was two of those money cases. You know, the ones that look like plastic briefcases.

Harry nodded. Rootboy was slapping his hands against the sides of the pin table and an electronic voice was saying, *Jackpot, Double Jackpot.* Rootboy whooped with joy and kept on flipping. The thin man continued.

Well the problem is that they're full of dye. For security. When

<62>

you open them you get sprayed with dye and the money's covered. So it's worthless.

Harry smiled.

You're sure about this?

The thin man tapped his fingers on the rim of his coffee cup, slid the glasses up the bridge of his nose again.

Yeah, I'm sure. We drove back here yesterday and took the cases into my garage. I knew about the dye, I'm not dumb. So I told him to wait in there until I'd made a few calls and found out the way to get around this. That's when I called up Davis and he told me to see you. Anyway, when I got back the fuckin' idiot had decided to try and open one of the cases himself. So he's fucking covered in the stuff. He looks like he's been boiled or something. He's as red as a fucking tomato.

Harry laughed. Can I take it that the two of you are not professionals?

The thin man ignored the remark. So you see we still have one case. If we could get into that then we'd be alright. It would've been worth it. Do you know how to do it?

Well, it's possible certainly. I can probably arrange it. I'll need time though. And I'm afraid that my associate, he jerked a thumb towards Rootboy, and I have a little business of our own to attend to that will keep us occupied for the next few days at the very least. If you see us back here in, say, five days then I'll try to have something sorted out.

The thin man scratched at his arm, raising up the sleeve of his teeshirt and exposing a crude blue tattoo.

Is that the best you can offer?

I'm afraid so. Of course you might be able to find somebody else to help you out but I don't think it's a good idea to just go asking around do you? From what I can make out you're not exactly, what I'd call, connected.

Okay. Okay. And how much will it cost?

<63>

It depends. It depends on how much you make. There'll be my consultation fee of course, and then a fee for technical services. I suppose we're looking at five K minimum. That's regardless of how much, or how little, is in the case. That's a flat fee with us having the option on 40% of the take on anything above that.

The thin man swallowed and then stood. He held out his hand and said that he'd look forward to seeing Harry again later, then walked quickly out of the cafe into the early morning sun. Rootboy came over and sat in his seat.

He's gone already. Is he coming back?

I very much doubt it. I think we're a little too expensive for him. Some people are so fucking greedy that they'll always go for the biggest percentage. Even if it's 100% of nothing with a shitload of trouble thrown in.

So, what was it all about?

Ha, nothing really. Amateurs is all. We're going to have to have a word with Davis. Fuck it. Harry raised his eyes to the ceiling. Where have all the class acts gone?

<64>

Goodbye Johnny

John. That was a long time ago. It seemed like forever. Sitting on daddy's knee. Singing. Bouncing up and down. *Johnny shall have a new bonnet, and Johnny shall go to the fair, and Johnny shall have a blue ribbon, to tie up his bonny brown hair.* A long time ago now. Before Dolores, before Jane. A long time gone from being plain John.

The last time Jane had seen her father was at Charing Cross station a year or so previously. Things had been getting to her, she was being suffocated by her family, her job and her friends. They all wanted to understand. At least they all said that they did but when it came right down to it they all found her moodswings and her erratic behaviour just that little bit too hard to handle and once some little thing went wrong then everything went wrong and it all degenerated into a screaming fit with whoever happened to be close to her at the time.

Her father's method of dealing with problems was to throw money at them. Always had been, from right back as far as she could remember. She could throw a tantrum as a child. Rolling in the aisles of a department store and her father would not only buy her the thing that he'd just that second said she couldn't have, but something to go along with it too. Scream loud enough and you shall receive. That's what she'd learned.

So when her father finally realised that his son was not like all of his friends' sons and was probably not ever going to be like any of his friends' sons he took the considered option of making available a large sum of money in the hope that Johnny would go off and tie up his bonny brown hair somewhere else. Anywhere else as long as it wasn't home.

John took the money, moved to Paris, invented another life and called that life Dolores. Then when Dolores finally ran out of

<65>

money and decided that coming back to London was the logical next step on the road to fortune and fame she called up her father, introduced herself to him and told him she was coming home and to pick her up at Charing Cross.

By the time the boat-train pulled in to the station she'd decided that she was making a big mistake. You can never go home. Wasn't that how it went. So she lifted her bag down on to the platform, wrapped her scarf around her face, put on her shades and shimmied right past her father, click-clacking heels across the concourse, the roll-a-bag trundling behind her. She was looking good. This mysterious beauty, a vision of Parisian elegance and sophistication. She stopped and lit a cigarette, glanced over at her father who was bobbing around looking up and down the platform. Jingling his car keys. Looking for Johnny. She made for the exit, got into a cab and told the man to drive.

Now Jane sat in front of the mirror doing her Snow White routine and pulling faces to keep away the wrinkles. Over her shoulder she could see Marie, with her hands on her hips, staring down at the bulging black mass of the 600 denier polyester Pierre Cardin roll-a-bag. Its top gaping open and clothes spilling over the sides.

Are you going to help me or are you just going to sit and stare at yourself?

What?

I said, can you come and help me with this stupid thing? Marie sat down on top of the bag while Jane came over and attempted to get the zip moving and the damn thing shut.

There's too much in here. We've got to lose some of it, Marie. I mean, do we really need all this?

Of course. We've got to be prepared. We've got to look good. I'm only thinking of you. It's the bag. It's too small.

Jane tugged at the zip but it wouldn't move. You know when I came back from Paris everything I owned was in this bag.

<66>

Everything. It's a big bag.

Marie squirmed on top, pushing down. Come on, now. Now. This time.

Jane fed a stray cotton dress strap back between the teeth of the zip and pulled again. Shit. Shit. Shit. She squealed and jumped backwards. It bit me. The fucking thing bit me. Look. It's broken my nail. Look at this. She held out her hand so Marie could see the snapped nail on her ring finger.

Alright, alright. Sorry. I'll go through it again. Marie got up off the bag and opened it. Clothes, magazines, make-up, cassettes and shoes came spilling out on to the floor. She started sorting them into piles. Essentials over here, almost essentials over here, not quite essentials over here and things we can just about get by without over there.

After five minutes Marie had decided that she could just about get by with only four pairs of shoes and that they could just about get by without her copies of *The Minnesota Tapes* and *The Genuine Basement Tapes* provided she had her copy of *Thin Wild Mercury Music* close at hand. Everything else had to stay. She carefully stacked it all in the bag and eased it shut. She pulled out the retractable towing handle and had a practice walk around the room, the castors rolling like thunder over the linoleum. Perfect.

<67>

Wreckology

When Ray woke, Lisa was already up and dressed. She carried a mug of coffee over to the bed. Ray yawned and sat up reaching forward to kiss Lisa.

What time is it baby?

Just after nine.

Ray sipped the coffee and mumbled.

What did you get up at this time for? We must've only been sleeping a couple of hours.

Habit I guess. I forgot I don't have a job to go to.

Lisa was sifting through a pile of albums that leaned up against the wall. She pulled a record from its sleeve and set it spinning on the turntable.

Hey, c'mon, do me a favour, turn it down a little will you? And throw me my shirt from over there. Ray pointed to the crumpled red heap that was hanging over one of the speakers. Lisa said that he couldn't wear it again, that it looked like a dish cloth and that he'd have to borrow something of hers. She pulled a white teeshirt from a drawer and tossed it over to him. He pulled on the shirt and threw back the bedclothes, stumbling out of the bed and past Lisa who made a grab for his naked backside. In the tiny kitchen area Ray started rattling around inside the cupboards, opening drawers.

What are you looking for?

He poked his head around the glass partition that separated the cooking area from the rest of the room.

Aspirins. Paracetemol. Anything. A hacksaw and I'll cut the fucking thing right off. I've got one killer headache.

Well you're not going to find any. You'll have to take it like a man.

Ray ran some water into the sink and splashed his face. He

<68>

dried his hands by running his fingers through his hair, using his nails as a comb. He picked up the bottle of whisky that they'd been working on the night before and climbed back into the bed. Kill or cure then. He poured the last finger of whisky into his coffee and lit a cigarette butt from the ashtray, instantly breaking into a coughing fit.

You're going to have to start slowing down old man, Lisa was laughing at him as he spluttered and tried to keep the coffee from spilling over him. That feeble body of yours just can't take the pace anymore.

Ray stopped coughing and took a sip from the mug then set it down.

Oh no? He leaped from the bed and grabbed Lisa, tickling her until she was screaming for mercy. As they struggled, they fell backwards into the record player sending the arm skidding across the album while the speakers howled in protest. Ray stopped tickling and held Lisa so they could listen to the sound of the stylus skating over the record label.

Sounds like you've been lifting records from the club last night. Doesn't sound any better the morning after though does it?

Ray let Lisa up and she righted the arm on the turntable, carefully returning the stylus to the start of the album. Then she climbed back into the bed with Ray and rested her head against his chest.

What's with all those eyes?

Lisa looked up at the ceiling.

I don't know. I was bored I guess. There was a big stain up there and it always bugged me. I figured it'd be more fun than painting it. Don't you like it? It isn't really finished.

Ray shifted in the bed and they both lay down and looked up at all the staring, unblinking eyes. I don't know. It's a little unusual that's all.

Cheaper than wallpaper though. They're like my guardian

<69>

angels, when you're not around.

Ray stroked Lisa's hair. I suppose that's one way of looking at it. You're funny alright, you know that.

Maybe. I don't know. Sometimes I just get ideas. I watched this film the other night on the TV. A French film. It was old. Black and white. I think it was called Infidelity. Have you ever seen it?

Can't say that I have.

Well this woman is having an affair and her husband finds out. Then she finishes the affair.

Doesn't sound like all that much to me.

No it wasn't. But the woman in the film, the one who was having the affair, she said this line. I thought about us. She said, 'Love's a bubble. When it touches earth, it's over.' Do you think that's what's going to happen to us?

I don't know. I don't think so. We can make sure it doesn't anyhow.

How are we going to do that?

Well Lisa, you and me, we'll never hit the ground.

The record had ended and they lay and listened to the sound of the traffic and to the chatter of children leaving for school. Ray drifted back to sleep and was woken by Lisa leaning over him. Telling him to wake up and asking him what time did he have to meet Rudi?

He opened an eye and mumbled: Twelve, why what is it now?

It's okay. You still have plenty of time. But you better get up and get ready.

Ray gathered up the rest of his clothes and started to dress.

Are you worried?

No, not really. He sat on the bed and put on his boots. To be honest I'm sort of glad. It's showed me that I've got to get it together. I was acting dumb and it was better that Rudi pulled me instead of the police.

But he's dangerous. You told me that yourself.

<70>

Yeah, he's dangerous. But what do I have to offer him? He's not going to get anything but cheap labour from me. If he wanted to hurt me, physically I mean, then he would've done it when he pulled me in. As it stands I figure that he'll just get me to run around for him. He has people already to do the big stuff. He can hardly trust me to manage anything major. He must already think I'm a useless fuck for letting him catch me.

Do you have to go?

Look, this is serious. I don't have to go. But if I don't, I can't stay either. And if I don't stick around here then I can kiss you goodbye.

But we could go together. Like I said last night, we could still go somewhere. Lisa had come over to the bed and was grasping Ray's hand. Shit. This is such a mess.

Ray stood and moved to the window.

I told you. We can't. We don't have nearly enough money. If we try and run with what we've got then we're just going to end up in a worse situation than we are already. At least here I know what I'm doing, or I thought I did. We'll ride this out, then pull in some money from somewhere even if I have to push for credit to start the thing up again. We'll go when we're ready and not before. I'll clean this mess up somehow.

He stood, staring out of the window and waited for Lisa to speak. For now he had nothing left to say on the matter. Lisa stayed silent. She'd bide her time.

In the yard of the house opposite was a wrecked silver Mercedes. The black vinyl roof had been crushed so that, on the driver's side, it was about a foot clear of the door panel. A huge V-shaped dent in the bonnet had forced the headlights to come together until they were virtually facing each other. The front tyres were flat and a pool of oil had collected beneath the busted engine and spread across the gravel. The last time Ray had been over, a Sunday afternoon, he remembered watching the owner

<71>

lovingly wax the bodywork. Only partly visible through the shattered windscreen was a white sign. From where he stood Ray couldn't make out what it said.

Hey what happened to that guy's Merc?

He had an accident. About a week ago.

What, and he's trying to sell it. In that condition?

Sell it? No, he died.

What's the sign say then?

Lisa stood next to Ray at the window, and looked down at the car. His wife put it there. She never saw the body. They wouldn't let her. There wasn't much left. She asked to have the car to remember him by. The sign says: What Drink Can Do.

Ray stared at the wreck. That's sick.

Maybe. But she says she's going to keep it there as a memorial. Everybody's been complaining. I don't know. I guess it's a little extreme.

Just after eleven o'clock, Ray walked out of the house closing the door quietly behind him. He was sure that Lisa was paranoid about her landlady. If he hadn't woken her the night before then she was either deaf as a post or, more likely, didn't give one either way. As he walked past the wreck of the Mercedes he took a close look at the sign and its careful, precise lettering and wondered what had been going through the woman's mind as she'd run the black marker over the card.

As he cut through an alley and onto a patch of waste ground that served as a play area for the neighbourhood kids, he tried in vain to get Lisa's teeshirt tucked into his trousers. It was too damn short and it kept riding up above his belt as he walked. His heels crunched on broken glass and he kept his eyes to the ground so as to avoid the larger pieces of debris.

Seeing the wreck had somehow reminded him of the time he

<72>

found a dead dog when he was a kid. It had been hit by a car and he, and some of his friends, had dragged the body from the side of the road into their secret place in a clump of weeds on a patch of waste ground like the one he was now crossing. They had prodded the dog's body with sticks until they had managed to work a hole in its side and then they had pulled out its guts with a hooked piece of wire. The stench had been terrible. As a final triumph over the animal, one of his friends had stuck two sticks into its eye sockets so that it resembled some kind of nightmare insect. Every day for a week they had returned to the body and watched it decay, its skin beginning to squirm as the maggots hatched out inside. Then they got bored and didn't go back for ages. When they finally returned all that was left was what looked like a rotten furry sack of bones. They buried the remains and, weeks later, Ray's friend, Declan, had dug them up and mounted the skull on the cow horn handlebars of his bike.

Then Ray thought of a book he'd read where a woman had kept the skull of her dead husband on the dressing table by the side of her bed. The wrecked car didn't seem so strange any more. Even the cut-out eyes made some kind of sense.

<73>

Loose Joints

Loose Joints came limping out of the newsagents, carrying a rolled up copy of The Sporting Life and bumped straight into Ray. It took a couple of seconds before they recognised each other then Loose Joints was grabbing Ray by the arms and saying, Ray, Ray, my man, it's been so damn long and how the fuck are you and it's good to see you.

Loose Joints, whose real name was Tommy Rourke, had been the best burglar Ray had ever seen. Short, slim with a mop of red hair tied back in a ponytail or worn up under the blue corduroy cap that Ray ribbed him about, saying that he looked like Donny Osmond, Loose Joints could get in anywhere, through the smallest of windows or narrowest of gaps, and the only way that anybody could figure he did it was by dislocating his shoulders and flopping through. Of course that wasn't what he did but it was how he'd got his name. Ray had worked B&Es with him for a time and he'd been a magician. One time, Tommy had somehow managed to pull a 26 inch FST TV through a skylight that had looked so small that Ray hadn't even attempted to climb through it. It was all in the angles, Tommy said, like playing pool or snooker. Know your angles and you'd be alright. One job that Tommy had done on his own, Ray had got tied up with something else and had to call off, he'd been disturbed by a nightwatchman as he was easing his way up a maintenance ladder on the side of a warehouse. Tommy jumped and got away but the fall shattered his ankle, resulting in a limp that meant the odds were stacked too much against him to continue his trade. Like he said, from then on in the angle was all wrong.

Ray had always felt guilty about that, about the busted ankle and the forced retirement of one of the best there ever was. If he'd been with him it might never have happened. Because of Ray's

<74>

guilt they'd lost touch with each other, not through any animosity but because, well, Ray just didn't know what to say to a man who, indirectly, he'd robbed of his livelihood. Now, seeing that same blue cap, a little frayed around the edges maybe, Ray wished that he had kept in touch. Loose Joints' greeting showed that he didn't harbour any grudges and, if Ray had thought about it, he should have known that he wouldn't. Loose Joints was a professional, and, as he often used to say when one of their plans didn't come off: Fuck it all, we've still got tomorrow. Last that Ray had heard of him he was playing the 'stolen jewellery' con on tourists on Oxford Street.

The two men walked on down the street towards the tube station.

So fuck it man, what's happening? Sorry I haven't been in touch but y'know... The sentence trailed off. Loose Joints flashed a look at his foot, kind of hopped on it. Skipped. Then said that he was doing fine and that Ray was a stupid dick to have let some dumb accident come between them and Ray stopped and looked at him face to face and then looked down and said, Yeah, I'm sorry man. Sorry about it all. They walked a little further and by the time they reached the station Loose Joints had told Ray how things were going fine for him, how he was moving on and gradually easing his way into doing something straight. How it took a great leap of faith but he was almost ready to make the commitment. They parted at the tube station with Ray explaining that he had a very important meeting and that he couldn't stop and talk like he wanted to but that he would give him a call just as soon as he had a minute and they'd have a few and he'd tell him about all the shit that was happening so that he could maybe get one of those angles on it. He wrote the phone number on a strip torn from the newspaper and they shook hands.

Ray sat in a carriage at the front of the tube and it shuddered and snorted like an animal as it moved off into the tunnel.

<75>

Opposite, a couple of tourist girls started comparing their shopping from the pile of bags at their feet. Good, expensive stuff that came in classy bags, all matt card, gold embossing and rope handles. He watched them going through the stuff, imagined following them back to their hotel, introducing himself. Good afternoon, my name is Ray Gardner. Could I possibly interest you in a guided tour of this beautiful city? They'd smile and say, Yes of course, that would be divine and he'd hail a cab and he'd show them around and then later, they'd get drinks brought up to their room and then they'd bathe together and he'd fuck them both on the hotel's kingsize. He had the taller girl blowing him, looking up at a painted ceiling, green velvet curtain, gold brocade, when he noticed that the train had stopped and they'd both got off.

He stared down at the floor. Thought about Lisa and felt ashamed for a couple of seconds. Station after station flew past and he felt his throat tighten and the base of his spine tingle as he reached his stop.

On the platform he watched the digital clock click to 11:53 as the train disappeared into the tunnel, gradually growing fainter until it sounded like a heartbeat. He rode the escalator to the street then turned into the narrow passage that led to Hades.

Painted across the brickwork above the reinforced steel door of the club was a giant pair of sunglasses and at the bridge of the peeling spectacles a neon sign in the shape of a nose that spelled out SHADES. At night the letters flashed in sequence but the first 'S' had been broken for as long as Ray could remember. Everybody called the club Hades and Rudi, the owner, was more than happy with that.

Ray stood in front of the steel door and pressed the bell. The red light of a security camera winked back at him and from somewhere inside the building a button was pressed and the door locks buzzed open. Ray pushed his way through the heavy door and walked into the strange stillness of the nightclub.

<76>

Queerfish

From where Ray stood in the foyer of Hades he could see the dancefloor naked under the house lights. Above the cigarette scarred flooring a mirrorball slowly revolved, its spotlight scattering tiny squares of light over empty tables and chairs. He heard a shout from behind him and turned to face a vinyl padded door set into the wooden panelled walls.

Gardner. Follow me.

The voice belonged to Frank, the man who'd telephoned, but Ray didn't get a glimpse of any more of him than the thick, gold-ringed fingers that beckoned him through the open doorway and then disappeared up the stairs. Ray followed and climbed a short flight of steps until he came to a door at the end of a hallway. When he reached it, the door opened and Frank's massive frame was barring his way. His blue and yellow tracksuit swelled at the arms where his muscles fought with the cotton. He was so wide that Ray couldn't see past him into the room. Reminded him of that comic book super villain, the Kingpin. Frank stood aside saying, Rudi will see you now and he stepped past Ray and closed the door behind him.

I'm so glad you could make it Ray.

Rudi was seated behind a large polished oak desk, the surface of which was covered with papers spilling out of a red wire tray. Three old style bakelite telephones, an ancient looking intercom and a carved wooden box in the shape of a small coffin jostled for space on the desk top. Behind the desk, on shelves, were the fishtanks and Ray's eyes were immediately drawn to them.

I like your fish, Rudi.

Good, I'm so pleased. If everything works out as I hope it will, you'll be getting to know at least one of them very well.

Rudi motioned towards the swivel chair that was placed in

<77>

front of the desk and Ray sat down. He slid the wooden box towards Ray. Cigarette?

Ray lifted the lid. Inside was a white china skull and, along the bottom of the velvet lined box, long menthol cigarettes arranged like the bones of a skeleton. Ray took a cigarette and placed it in his mouth then reached into his pocket for a light.

Allow me. Rudi pointed a small snub-nosed handgun at Ray. Ha, ha, don't worry. He pulled the trigger and a long butane flame leapt from the barrel. Ray leaned forward and took a light.

Cigarettes are very dangerous Ray. Very bad for you. Rudi reached under some of the papers on the desk and pushed the ashtray over. Ray looked at the bones in the plastic and flicked a little ash from the tip of his cigarette into it. He leaned back in the chair.

So what is it that you want?'

We'll get to that. All in good time. It doesn't pay to be too eager. You'd like a drink? Rudi pushed a button on the intercom and a minute later Frank came in carrying a tray on which was set a bottle of Chivas Regal, a tumbler and a tall glass of coke on top of which floated a scoop of ice cream. Frank set the tray on the desk and backed out of the room without saying a word.

Rudi took the coke float and sipped, flicking out his tongue to catch the brown foam that caught on his top lip. Pour yourself a drink. I'm afraid I no longer drink alcohol in the afternoons. It makes me sleepy. I thought you may prefer it.

Ray picked up the bottle and poured himself a measure. This encounter was turning out to be more unpleasant than he'd imagined. There was something vaguely obscene about the way Rudi was slurping on the coke float. It reminded him of the barman drooling over the hula-girls. He watched Rudi run his tongue around the edge of his glass scooping up the melting ice-cream. With his mouth ringed with foam, he started to speak.

So, I was talking to a friend of yours recently. That Harry. He's

<78>

a funny guy. He was trying to sell me a new business idea. Fuck-a-grams. Ha. Stupid really. I told him, I already have all the girls, in all the permutations that I need. I don't need another gimmick. He hadn't thought it through at all. That guy he had with him though, he thought it was a great idea. What's his name, I forget. You know, the one with the scar running down here, Rudi ran his finger down his cheek, picking up a little melted ice cream as it passed his lips.

Rootboy.

Ah, that's the man. Stupid name. Why's he called that?

Ray sipped on his drink, he was watching the fish swimming around in the tanks behind the desk and wondering why Harry hadn't mentioned that he'd been talking to Rudi. For that matter, how did Rudi know that he knew him? Then he got an uneasy feeling as he remembered the talk of the burned out club and Rootboy muttering Fantastic! It was fucking fantastic, and then Harry's thick roll of fifties. They had to be working for him. He thought about asking outright but then thought better of it and just answered the question.

It's to do with the size of his dick.

Rudi laughed. What?

He claims his dick is so big that the girls say he's putting down roots. I think it's all in his head. It started off as a joke, I think he even started it, and I guess it just stuck.

Roots! That's good, very good. Rudi's body quivered as he laughed.

Ray leaned forward and set his glass down. Lying open on the desk he could see the glossy paper of a skin mag. Speciality stuff by the looks of it but mundane. Looking at it upside down he could make out a girl being pissed on by three men and, in another frame, the same girl squatting over a man and defecating into his open mouth. Underneath each photograph was a set of captions with national flags next to each piece of text: for people

<79>

so illiterate they didn't recognise their own language in its written form, Ray assumed. When he looked up Rudi was staring back at him.

. What you did the other night was very stupid Ray. It could've caused me a lot of trouble. Now, if you'd have asked, explained the situation to me then I could have found an opening for you. But, you see, I can't just let people wander in off the street and start taking my custom away, ha, or even one of my customers as you seemed to be trying to...

Ray jumped in: You know that's shit. That would've happened to that girl whether I'd been here or not. There was nothing wrong with the stuff I had.

Yes, well maybe. But that isn't the point. You see I don't allow outside operators. I like to know what's happening at all times. Who's where and what they're doing and when they're doing it. I run a tight ship.

Ray was getting bored of all the talk, he wanted Rudi to get to the point. Tell him what he wanted from him.

Look, have you just called me in here to give me a bollocking because if you have then I'll say I'm sorry and that it won't happen again and perhaps I can go.

He started to rise from his seat.

Rudi raised his hand and told him to sit back down. He rocked in his chair and kicked his feet up onto the desktop. He was wearing a brand new pair of alligator shoes and Ray could see that the tan leather soles didn't even have a scratch on them.

It isn't quite as simple as that Ray. I need you to do something for me. Just a little thing to wipe the slate clean. You see if I didn't get something from you then I'd soon find that word had got around and people would start taking liberties. Before you know it the situation would get out of hand. What I want you to do is quite straightforward. Very little risk, I'll even pay you for your time. And, if you like the work, perhaps we can come to some

<80>

arrangement. Make it regular. I'm always on the lookout for good people.

Ray shifted in his seat. Regular? There was nothing regular about the way Rudi worked. It'd be like working with a razor at your neck, ready to slice an extra smile if you swayed so much as an inch from the fat man's path.

What if I refuse to do it? Whatever it is.

Rudi stared blankly back at him: Well, that wouldn't be the right answer.

Okay, so what is it that you want?

Well first, I want you to watch a film with me. Rudi opened a drawer in the desk and took out a TV remote control. He pointed it over Ray's shoulder. Ray swivelled in his chair so that his back was to the desk. Fixed high up in the corner, to the left of the door was a TV set with a video recorder on a shelf below it.

The video picture came into focus on the large TV screen. A huge glass bowl filled with water hung in the centre of a room, suspended from the ceiling by four lengths of chain. Men in evening dress were sat on circles of chairs around the bowl, reading from folded cards like menus or talking among themselves. Waitresses flitted in and out of frame refilling long stemmed wine glasses. The lights dimmed until only a spotlight illuminated the bowl. Ray caught sight of Rudi in the front row, his bulk stuffed into a dinner suit, his face red as though his bow tie was strangling him.

The camera zoomed in on the bowl as it swung, ever so slightly, on its chains. Two men approached it, each carrying a small glass jar. They held the jars out and touched them together like they were making a toast and then they turned to face the camera. Inside each of the jars a small brightly coloured fish was swimming round and round. Carefully, the two men lowered the fish into the large bowl and backed away. The fish swam at each other, flashing long, graceful tails and fins as they nipped one

<81>

another. For some minutes, the camera focused on the fish as they ducked and darted in the bowl. Although there was no soundtrack to the video Ray judged by the movements of the men at the rear of the frame that they were shouting encouragement. Strange, there seemed to be very little to get excited over.

Rudi fast-forwarded the picture. When he pressed play one of the fish was lifted from the water, apparently motionless. The other swam around and around, showing off its fins and beautiful red colouring. The camera zoomed past the tank and focused on Rudi in the front row. He was smiling, arms folded contentedly. Rudi clicked off the tape and the screen went blank. When Ray turned to face him again he was wearing that same broad grin of ragged teeth.

I don't expect you to appreciate the finer points of the sport, Ray. But what you have just seen are the highlights of a memorable contest. A match that earned me many thousands of pounds.

Ray looked puzzled. Before he could speak Rudi continued.

Beta Splendens. Siamese fighting fish. Cheaper to run than a racehorse but potentially as lucrative. Pound for pound that is. Rudi laughed.

I'm sorry I don't understand. Why did you show me the film?

I thought you might be interested. I like my people to know the background to the work I set them.

Ray poured himself another glass of Chivas Regal and sipped on it. I'm still not with you.

You see Ray. Myself, and some of my friends and associates like a little sport now and then. This, he gestured to the TV and then to the fishtanks, is how we relax. It's so much cleaner than dog-fighting don't you think? So much more civilised.

So where do I fit in?

I want you to drive for me.

And...?

<82>

And nothing. You see Ray, I have a very big contest coming up, there's a lot of money resting on it. An awful lot. It's become something of a grudge match.

So where is it? Where do I have to go?

Well Ray, this is the best part. It's in Amsterdam. I want you to drive my fish to Amsterdam.

Ray looked at the fishtanks. For the first time he noticed the small jar on the top shelf and the dull little fish it contained. He looked back at Rudi who was idly picking at his fingernails with a mother-of-pearl handled stiletto. Is this for real?

Of course.

Will you be going to this contest then?

I will. But you see, the fish will need a day or so to get over its journey. A day or so after you've delivered I'll fly over. I'm afraid your involvement ends when you hand over the fish. The contest itself is very exclusive. Invitation only and, I'm sorry, but you're not invited. Another cigarette? Rudi flipped open the lid of the coffin and Ray reached over and took one.

Wouldn't it be easier to just fly the fish over? Why do you want me to drive it?

I'll be honest Ray. Like I said, I like my people to have the background information. What I'm asking you to do is not, strictly, legal. That's not to say that you're going to get into trouble. There are the little matters of export licenses to get this kind of thing out of the country. We have always found in the past that the customs men are so much more stringent at the airports. This way, if you'll excuse me, I'm certain that you'll just sail through.

Ray nodded. The whole deal stank. Okay. So, say that I agree to do it...

No Ray, let's not say you agree. You do agree. You have no choice.

Okay then, so when do you want me to do it?

<83>

That's better. Well today is Wednesday right. You're to have the fish delivered by Saturday afternoon. I've taken the liberty of booking you a cross-channel ticket for early Friday morning. That will give you plenty of time to get sorted out. Shall we say that I'll see you tomorrow? Same time? I'll have somebody call you and let you know where to meet and I'll have Frank arrange a vehicle.

Ray stood up, ready to leave, then turned back to face Rudi. You said you were going to pay me for this. How much?

Rudi laughed: Of course, the money. Well I was thinking of around a grand up front to cover your incidental expenses and then a further grand on delivery. It would be more but you see you still owe me don't you? We can't forget that. By the way, feel free to take someone along with you if you wish. I'm sure you probably would anyway so I may as well say that it's okay. We may as well be honest with each other. I'll have a hotel booked for you. A double room. Once you've delivered you can do as you please. Enjoy yourself.

Rudi reached across the desk to shake hands. The fat man's grip tightened and a wicked smile played on his lips. He was staring at Ray with the same icy intensity that he had shown when he'd pulled him in the first time. The whole thing might have sounded crazy but that look showed that Rudi was deadly serious. Ray pulled his hand free and walked to the door. He turned the handle as Rudi spoke.

Ray, just one more thing.

Rudi was again playing with the knife, spinning it between his fat fingers. No fuck-ups.

Ray let himself out and went down the stairs. Frank was waiting for him in the foyer and shepherded him out on to the street.

<84>

If This Was A Rocketship...

Somebody had passed out in the lift and the stench from the man's soiled pants and the angle at which he lay meant that Ray had chosen the stairs as the more favourable route to Loose Joints' flat. Some choice. He climbed the stone stairs, reading the walls as he went, all random graffiti and spray-can tags. On the wall of the first half-landing was a beautifully painted figure, some ten feet across, arms outstretched and wearing a star covered cloak of blue and green. Letters written in the lightning bolts that emanated from his wand spelled out WIZARD in vibrant reds and purples. Ray stopped to admire the figure. Even though some less enterprising artists had scrawled their tags over parts of it in thick, black squiggles, it was still something to see. He walked on and felt the cuff of his trousers catch some liquid and he looked down and saw that he'd stepped in a puddle of urine. He shook his trouser leg and climbed the next staircase, cursing as he stepped carefully over broken syringes and used condoms. As he reached the top he kicked out at the crushed half of a lemon that lay on the top step and sent it flying back down the staircase, landing with a splat in the pool of urine.

The sign on the landing read Huston House Flats 23-33 and Ray checked the scrap of paper that he'd written the address on. He remembered Loose Joints saying that it was the one with the red door and that there was a windowbox on the flat next to it. When Ray had called after leaving Hades, Loose Joints had seemed genuinely pleased, relieving Ray's fears that he'd been embarrassed into giving him his number. He walked down the landing, looking out on the courtyard below where a group of kids raced around on mountain bikes and a woman sat on a bench watching a young child climb a painted yellow steel frame in the shape of a spaceship.

<85>

He passed a windowbox full of dried up brown plants with a toy windmill planted amongst them, and reached a red door with a white plastic 29 fixed to it. From inside the flat came the incessant beat of a techno track and Ray waited until the music had finished before he rattled the letterbox. Loose Joints poked his head around the curtains in an adjacent window, nodded at Ray and then came and opened up the door beckoning him inside.

He led Ray through into a living room littered with baby toys and plastic building bricks. Loose Joints grabbed an armful of fluffy animals from the sofa and threw them across the room onto the empty cot under the window and told Ray to sit if he was staying. The place smelled, a mixture of urine and disinfectant. From the baby, Ray hoped, and not from his trouser leg. He looked over at the mantelpiece where there was a photograph of Loose Joints, in his blue cap, holding a baby dressed in a pair of orange dungarees. Loose Joints saw what he was looking at and picked up the picture and carried it over to him.

You won't know will you? That's my son Cathal. It's a little old now, he'll be a year come next month.

Ray held the picture as carefully as if he'd been holding the boy himself, looking closely at the baby and at Loose Joints' beaming smile. I had no idea. Congratulations. He handed the picture back and shook Loose Joints' hand.

Yeah, it's good. I read somewhere that having kids is like planting trees. It's lumber for the future. I guess what they mean is that when you get old they keep you warm, in a manner of speaking. We're going to have a whole forest of them. He's a darling. He's out with Caitlin at the minute. They've gone over to see my mother.

Loose Joints placed the picture back on the mantelpiece then walked through into the kitchen. He returned, swinging four cans of lager from their plastic collar. He threw a can over to Ray then went over to the stereo and and put on another disc adjusting the

<86>

volume so that he could be heard over the music.

So Ray, it's been a while. Will you tell me what's happening?

Ray recounted his meeting with Rudi then went back and told how he'd come to be in this position in the first place. Loose Joints sat on the floor by the stereo swigging from the can and looking serious.

So you see, I'm stuck aren't I? I have to do it. I'm worried though, that even if everything goes to plan, when I get back Rudi is going to think that I'm on his team. He's going to want me to pull all kinds of shit for him all the time.

Loose Joints crushed his empty can and reached for another. He cracked it open and took a long drink. Shit. I don't know. This fish thing. Fuck. People do that? Seriously. That sounds fucked up to me. But then, think about it. If it's money that you want, if he's prepared to pay you two grand for this when, as you said yourself, you owe him, then think how much he'll pay you when you've cleared the debt. It'll only take a year or so, probably less, before you and Lisa have enough to move on wherever you want to go.

Yeah but that's the point. It's because of this sort of thing that I want to move on. I'm sick of it all. I'm getting too old. When you and me used to go out it was fun. Hell, it was easy money. A little risky but we were always okay, except I guess...

You're not still bothered about my ankle? Loose Joints slapped his hand against his leg. Occupational hazard. It wasn't like you pushed me or forced me to do the job in the first place.

Exactly. No one forced us to do anything. This way I'm being forced. I'm not in control, somebody else will make all the decisions.

So how was it going before all this? You said you'd got enough money together to set yourself up. I didn't think drugs were your line anyway?

Well no, not really. I spent a few months here and there. Simple

<87>

burglaries mostly, a few cars. Small change. It took a while but I got it together. It's all gone now though. Drugs seemed like easy money. I never had the bottle to go face to face on a hold-up.

Loose Joints took a bottle of Jamesons from the sideboard and poured a couple of measures. He handed one to Ray and then sat down beside him.

You know what? I think I can help you out.

How?

You know me, right? I know people. I get on with people. There's a guy I've known for a while. He runs a little import business. He's offered me this job a few times but I've never taken it. Maybe you might want to?

Ray stood up and walked over to the window, he picked up a blue fur rabbit from the cot and passed it from hand to hand. Uh, I don't know. If you haven't taken it there must be something wrong with it. What exactly would I have to do?

The reason I haven't taken him up on it is that I have other people to think about now, not just myself. That's why I'm sticking to stuff like selling the necklaces. I quit dreaming of the big score when Cathal came along. The way it is now I know that he needs a comfortable father more than he needs a heap of money and a father that's locked up for years on end… Shit Ray you're nervous.

Ray looked at his hands. He had the toy rabbit in a stranglehold. Yeah, I guess I am. He dropped the rabbit back into the cot. So are you going to tell me what the job is?

Yeah, right. It's neat because you won't even have to go out of your way. It ties in with the fish deal. This Dutch guy I know arranges E to be brought over from Holland. Stacks of the stuff. The deal he offered me was to pick up a consignment and drive it back. He has ways of getting it through all but the toughest border checks. You get paid a tenth of the value of what you bring over. So we're talking a minimum of ten grand. Any less and it's

<88>

not worth your while. He offered me the option of twice the cash value in gear so, theoretically, you could make twenty or thirty grand at least.

Ray lit a cigarette and stared out of the window. I don't know, I'll have to think about it.

Sure. I'm not forcing you. Take your time. Hey, can you open the window? I don't like smoke in the house. You know with the kid sleeping in here.

Ray opened the window and flicked his cigarette out. He asked Loose Joints where he'd met this guy and Loose Joints told him how a mutual acquaintance at this drinking club in Soho had introduced the Dutch guy to him one time when he'd been over on business and how he'd run in to him a couple of times since at the same place. Ray thought it over. Up to now, at least before, he'd been prepared to go with Loose Joints on almost anything. Almost always turned out alright before. It's sounding promising. I don't know. This has been a fucking crazy day.

Ha, you're right there. I can't believe that thing about the fish. That is fucking crazy.

They sat and talked with Loose Joints providing a soundtrack of pumping house music. When Ray complained that the tracks all sounded the same, Loose Joints said that he could say the same about rock'n'roll or blues. And anyway it's all music and this is good like Roy Orbison is good, like Elmore James is good. You understand? Every one of the Big O's numbers sounds the same, every one of Elmore James sounds the same. He sang out the intro to *Dust My Broom*. But they have feel. And this has feel. You get it? It's there man, I'm telling you. Listen. And he spun another side.

At four o'clock Loose Joints started tidying up the empty cans in preparation for his wife and son's return. Ray took it as a cue to leave and said that he'd call when he'd decided whether or not he wanted to try for the job and, whatever, he'd keep in touch.

<89>

On his way across the courtyard Ray thought about how many miles twenty grand would buy. How far away from all this it would take them. He passed the spaceship climbing frame and tapped its yellow metal tubes. Wishing for a second it was real. Wishing he could climb on board.

<90>

No Smoking

The plane took off two hours late so that Queen Jane Approximately and Absolutely Sweet Marie had ended up waiting at the airport for some four hours which was, as Jane pointed out, more than twice as long as the bitchin' flight was going to take. Marie ordered a small bottle of wine from the stewardess and started on the pile of glossy fashion mags that she'd bought. Jane had her headphones on and was watching a bad movie about a group of kids that had lost their pet dog and were desperately scouring suburban streets trying to find it. It wasn't really grabbing her. She loathed dogs. Shit-machines. That's all they were. She hoped the kids never found it though she doubted that was going to happen.

A young girl, Jane guessed she was four or five, kept peeping over the seat in front. Sticking her tongue out. Jane stuck her tongue out back, then the kid's father turned around and started to apologise, took one look at Jane and Marie and stopped mid-sentence, grabbed the girl and buckled her into her seat. Jane took off her headphones and turned to Marie, asking her if she could look at one of the magazines.

Sure, any of them. Take one.

What are you reading anyway?

Marie passed over the magazine she was looking at. Pointed at the side bar. Look at this one will you. Unbelievable. It's a roundup of news stuff. Odd things from around the world. Check this one out.

Jane started reading the piece that Marie had pointed at. 'Rumania: A man whose wife had told him that she had given up smoking was today charged with her murder. The man returned home early from work and caught his wife smoking a cigarette after she had told him that she had quit. He battered her to death

<91>

with the glass ashtray that she had been using. (Reuters).'

Then she started laughing.

Shit. I don't believe that at all.

Yeah, well it's in the magazine. It must be true. Look. Reuters. She prodded the page. That's the proof.

Okay. So what was his name? What was her name? Where was it in Rumania? What brand of cigarettes was she smoking? I mean. It's important.

Marie took a pack of Silk Cut out of her bag and offered the pack to Jane. They lit up and watched the other passengers start glaring at them, pretending to cough.

Marie laughed then turned to Jane and told her to put on her crash helmet because the steward was on his way.

<92>

Dead Flowers

So when I came in I found the little shit with her. Of all the people he could've been fucking it had to be that bitch didn't it? So I grabbed her clothes from the floor, she had these horrible, purple nylon knickers with white lace on them, dead tacky, and I just flung them out the fucking window. Right out into the road. He said, 'Honey, honey, it's not what you think!' The cunt, what was I supposed to think when I come in and all I can see is his white backside pumping up and down and the bitch underneath him going Oooooh! and Aaaaah, yes!

'It's not what you think!' He didn't even miss a stroke when he said it. That's a fucking joke isn't it? So I picked up the TV, we've got one those little portables, it's light, I could pick it up easily, and I threw it at them. Hit him on the back, yeah, just about here. Hope it fucking broke, too. Then I just walked out.

The woman's arms were folded, forcing her breasts to swell out of the V neck of her red lycra dress. Her friend listened intently, nodding her head, then she tapped her on the elbow and pointed out that it was their turn at the counter.

Ray and Lisa had just come from seeing a triple bill of old movies at a dilapidated rep cinema where the sound of a train running into or out of the nearby mainline station had succeeded in drowning out much of the dialogue.

They'd seen Bogart get a face change and hang out with Lauren Bacall in Dark Passage. Then Aldo Ray getting chased all over by a gang of hoods for a murder he didn't commit in Nightfall. Then they'd stayed awake through *The Moon In The Gutter* until someone with a fat head had decided to sit right in front of them blocking out the sub-titles. An hour gone and they'd decided that they didn't really care about what happened to Kerrigan. The film was still playing when they left. Ray had read the book in any

<93>

case and filled Lisa in with the story as they walked out of the cinema. Now they were standing in the queue for some fried chicken at a nearby take-away. They waited for the two women to be served and then ordered their food.

Distant thunder rolled in the sky echoing the sound of the trains. Rain was coming down in sheets and cars hissed along the street, their headlights bouncing yellow beams off the water on the road.

Ray pulled Lisa into the doorway of a discount bookstore, that had 'Mind Your Heads. Our Prices Are Low' painted on its window, so that they could eat the chicken out of the rain. People hurried past them, fighting with umbrellas or holding newspapers over their heads, hastened by the weather, their quick steps making them look like they were in a speeded up slapstick comedy.

What have you decided? Lisa bit into a chicken leg, a bead of grease dribbled down her chin and she mopped it up with a paper tissue.

I'm going to do it. I'll call Tommy first thing, see if he can sort it out in time.

You're sure?

Sure, I'm sure. This is our chance. One shot, one stroke of luck and we're there.

So what time are we leaving on Friday? Lisa tossed a chicken bone to the ground.

I'll find out tomorrow. I don't know though. Maybe you shouldn't come. Maybe I should go on my own.

But Ray...

What's the use of us both getting pulled if things go wrong? There's no sense in us both going.

Lisa waved a chicken leg in front of her face. Almost prodded Ray with it. This is some kind of man's gotta do what a man's gotta do bullshit, isn't it? Big macho male going out foraging

<94>

while the little woman stays at home. Shove it Ray. I'm coming.

Ray wiped his hands on a paper tissue then wadded it with the remains of his food and drop-kicked the bundle into the road where the tyres of a blue transit van crushed it into a soggy mess. Okay, well how about this? You come over with me and the stupid fucking fish. Then if I get the deal fixed with Loose Joints, I give you the money for the flight back and you meet me back here. If I'm coming back loaded it'd be better to be on my own. Borders are nowhere near as strict as they used to be but I can't risk you getting caught if something goes wrong. I'd never forgive myself.

The rain had eased to a steady drizzle and they stepped back out onto the pavement and headed for the train station. A group of whores huddled under a bus-stop, wet and bedraggled, mascara running around sad, pin eyes. The woman in the red dress was with them, handing out french fries from a crumpled paper bag.

Slumped on the stairs to the underground was a heavily tattooed man, the right sleeve of his sodden, black suit jacket rolled up. In his left hand he held a torn can of cider and was dragging the thin, jagged metal across his right forearm. He muttered to himself each time the can sliced the skin and drops of blood fell, flowering in the rainwater at his feet. Ray and Lisa stepped past him and into the dry warmth of the station.

<95>

Sweet Thursday

Thursday morning and Ray woke to find that the rain had leaked through the skylight in the kitchen, collecting in a puddle on the table and then dribbling across the formica to finally create a dark, spreading stain on the carpet. He got a cloth from the sink and wiped the table top. On the skylight he could see a string of water beads suspended along one of the seams in the glass, quivering, ready to drop. He laid down some sheets of newspaper over the damp patch and then busied himself making coffee and toast for Lisa who was, unusually, still asleep.

He peeked around the bedroom door while he waited for the kettle to boil. She lay there, wrapped in the tangled sheet, her legs and arms exposed, looking like a Roman goddess. He gently closed the door and then went over to the telephone.

After smoothing out the scrap of paper on the window-sill, he dialled Loose Joints' number and told him that he was prepared to try it. It took a couple of seconds for Loose Joints to remember what 'it' was, but when he did he just said, Sweet. That's sweet, Ray. I'll try and get hold of him this morning and get it sorted. Ray told Loose Joints that he'd be in his flat all day and to call as soon as he heard anything. He slipped a cassette into the machine and then went back into the kitchen and finished making breakfast.

<96>

99.9%

No matter how fucked the deal with the fish was, whatever came of it, at least Ray knew he was going to score with Loose Joints. He'd come back to him within an hour of his call and had set up a meeting with his connection in Amsterdam. The only condition his contact made was that Loose Joints had to be there, in person, to make the introductions. Loose Joints had said that sure, it was cool with him to spend a couple of days in Holland, no worries on that. But that Ray had to understand that he was only going as a tourist and that after they'd made the contact and Ray had taken delivery of the goods, he was out of there and would make his own way back to London where Ray could lavish a little 'thank you' on him when he got back himself. Ray had agreed to all of this. He was set to make a minimum of twenty grand with, as Loose Joints explained, the possibility of much more if the man thought that he felt safe. From Ray's way of thinking it seemed the logical thing to do was to carry as much as could be comfortably concealed in the car. If he was pulled in, it wouldn't matter if it was for one hundred or one hundred thousand. Loose Joints had assured him that they'd push for something serious and that, 99.9 per cent, they'd get it.

Now, Ray was sitting at a wooden table on the deck of a docked boat on the Thames. Late afternoon, Rudi having put back the meeting because of other unforeseen circumstances that Ray didn't ask about and didn't want to know about. He sipped at a glass of vodka and lemonade and looked down at the dirty, grey water wondering how many fish were swimming in it. As Rudi had requested in the telephone message, Ray was seated at the table farthest away from the little covered bar, and far away from any of the other drinkers. He watched a glass sided boat cruise by. The tourists crowded up against its windows, pointing

<97>

and taking pictures, reminded him of fish trapped in an overcrowded aquarium. Shit, everything seemed to remind him of fish.

A seagull eyed him from the railings, tilting its head one way, then the other like some inept feathered Casanova on the pull. Beady eyes. Seagulls seemed to have become like pigeons, rats and cockroaches. Everywhere. Some genius evolution. Persistent. Resistant. Like pigeons, rats and cockroaches, seagulls pissed him off. Ray picked up a butt from the ashtray and flicked it at the gull. The butt sailed past the bird over the rail and the seagull slow-flapped after it.

To his right were the Houses of Parliament. As he heard the chimes begin for four o'clock he looked over at the white, iron walkway that lead from the Embankment to the boat and saw Rudi and Frank coming down on to the deck. Rudi was wearing a rust coloured suit and a beige hat. In his hand he held a black leather case, like a bowling bag.

Frank walked over to the bar and Rudi came over to Ray's table and set the bag down on the green painted deck and took off his hat. He reached into his pocket for a cigar, lit it and then spoke.

Good timekeeping Ray, I'm impressed. If there's one thing I hate it's a poor timekeeper. Well, there's lots of things I hate but... y'know. Rudi laughed.

Frank arrived from the bar and placed an orange juice in front of Rudi and handed Ray a glass of whisky, then took his own drink and sat at the next table.

I'm not good enough for him to sit with huh? Ray drained his vodka and started on the whisky.

No Ray, it's just so that no-one else comes and sits next to us. We won't be keeping you a minute. Rudi reached down and opened the bag. He carefully lifted out a black package and placed it on the table in front of Ray. Here she is then, Ray, take

<98>

good care of her.

Ray reached out and touched the object. It was the same size and shape as the jar he'd seen in Rudi's office but it was completely covered in thick, black rubber. He dug his fingernail into the covering and felt it give a little, it had to be at least a half inch thick. The top was also sealed with rubber and a little excess adhesive had set hard at the seam. Ray picked up the container and tilted it slightly. He felt the weight inside it shift as though it was not quite full of water. He set it back down and looked at Rudi.

How can it breathe in there? There aren't any holes.

Rudi smiled. Think about it. It's a fish Ray, it doesn't need to breathe. This is a specially designed protective container. I would suggest that you position it in the boot of the car, wedge it in tightly against the spare wheel. Of course if you have somebody travelling with you, you could always get them to hold it all the way. The most important thing is that it doesn't get damaged in any way. Do you intend to bring somebody along with you? How about that girl of yours?

Ray continued to stare at the container and said to Rudi that he was planning to go on his own. There didn't seem to be any point in telling him something he didn't need to know. He particularly didn't want Rudi to get even a hint that he was planning to do anything else at all beyond handing over the fish while he was away.

Rudi put the container back into the bag and passed it over the table to Ray.

Inside the bag you'll find the location of the car Frank has got for you and the keys. It's on a meter about a five minute walk from here so don't hang around. There's an envelope in there too with the first part of your payment and the rest of your instructions. Everything is made painfully clear. When you return you're to come to the club and Frank will settle up with you.

<99>

Now, we really must get on.

Rudi stood and placed his hat back on his head and tucked in his shirt that had come loose around his belly while he'd been seated. He turned and walked back towards the gangway, Frank at his heels.

Ray positioned the bag so he could feel it on the deck between his feet. There was nobody near him but he knew how easy it was to get a bag away from somebody who wasn't paying attention.

Earlier when he'd said goodbye to Lisa he'd told her that she might as well get her stuff packed and start checking out those maps because when they came back from this trip they'd soon be away on the next one for good. Lisa had been talking about going to Italy or Spain. Renting a little villa on the coast where she could maybe get some work in a bar or hotel and they could live on what she earned and keep their money for travelling on or for the winter when there wouldn't be any work. Ray had been angling for them to go to America but this villa deal sounded fine and when he said that he figured they might even make a big enough score to set up their own place it sounded even sweeter. He didn't think this was likely, he doubted he'd get enough for anything like that and had only said it because he'd got carried away by Lisa's excitement but she'd taken to it and had even started thinking up names for the place. But twenty grand as a minimum stake was enough to get them started.

He reached down into the bag and opened up the envelope. Counted the money, all crisp fifties. Took one out, examined it. Wouldn't put it past Rudi to slip him some duds. Then he checked the departure time on the ticket and figured on when they should be leaving. They could spend the rest of the day getting things ready then lounge around at his flat and leave in the middle of the night. Plenty of time to get there for the first boat of the morning.

As a barman came over to clear the tables of Frank's empty glass and Rudi's untouched fruit juice, Ray finished up the whisky

<100>

and looked at his watch. It was time to go and get Loose Joints.
It was time to move.

<101>

Big Road Blues

Ray hit the horn again and looked up at Loose Joints' flat. Loose Joints came to the window carrying his son. He waved and then held up his hand indicating that he'd be five minutes and Ray waved back to the boy who was copying his father's actions. When they'd moved away from the window Ray reached over to the glove compartment where he'd stashed the envelope. Inside were the ferry tickets, the address of the hotel that Rudi had booked him into and a phone number that he was to call when he arrived. Ray took the money from the envelope and put it in his inside jacket pocket where he could feel the edges of the bundle digging into his armpit. He checked the time of the sailing on the tickets again, then returned the envelope to the glove box.

While he waited for Loose Joints he slotted a cassette into the car's system and bounced the sound around the speakers for a while with the balance control. When he got bored of that he started on the electric windows, matching the speed of the glass on the passenger side with that on the driver's.

When Loose Joints finally tapped on the window to be let into the car, Ray had adjusted his seat to a reclining position and was staring up out of the sun roof at the black clouds that were spilling across the sky like blotting paper soaking up ink.

Loose Joints was wearing white Levis and a black leather jacket and had his hair in a pony tail. In one hand he held his blue cap and in the other a small canvas bag that he tossed into the back seat as he climbed in.

Ready then? Ray started up the engine and put the car in gear.

Sure thing. Hey, Ray this is a nice motor. Loose Joints adjusted his seat as they moved out into the traffic, pushing it back so he could stretch out his legs.

Yeah, it's perfect isn't it? Flash but not so flash that it'll draw

<102>

attention to itself and not so beat up that it looks like we're completely skint.

Loose Joints reached over and picked up a piece of white card from the dash. Written across it were the words: PRIEST ON VISIT, ST MARY'S PARISH CHURCH. What the fuck is this? he laughed.

Ray laughed with him. I don't know. The car was on a meter when I picked it up. I guess it was some kind of extra insurance that it wouldn't get clamped or towed if I didn't get to it in time.

Loose Joints stared at the sign, shook his head, then put his window down and threw it out into the street.

We're going to go and hang out at my place for a few hours. Lisa's there now. Then we'll just take a leisurely drive down to the ferry in the morning. You got your passport?

Loose Joints feigned some crazy patting of his pockets, wrestling with his bag, going, Oh shit, shit. Oh shit. I don't... Then, Yeah Dad, I've got my passport. Why're we going on the ferry anyway? Hasn't this Rudi guy heard about that tunnel? Jesus. Ferries are like dinosaurs.

I don't know. I think he figures because it's new and all, they're going to be more stringent at the customs or something. But fuck. It's only a stupid fish anyway.

So where's this valuable fish then? Loose Joints asked as they crawled to a halt behind an endless queue of vehicles.

In the boot.

In the boot! Are you sure it'll be alright in there? Don't you think we should have it up front with us? I'd like to have a look at the little fucker.

You can't see it anyway. It's in this special container that's covered in rubber. It's all sealed up.

I've been thinking Ray. What happens if we get stopped. I mean, is it legal to transport fish? Don't they have some kind of quarantine laws for animals?

<103>

I'm not sure. Rudi said something about needing a license but I guess with this kind of thing, the worst that could happen if it was found would be they'd confiscate it and maybe slap a fine on us. I mean it's only one fucking fish after all.

Yeah, ha, I suppose we could always swallow the thing like those guys do with the goldfish.

Ray laughed. I don't know. I wouldn't fancy doing that. It's usually a carved up piece of carrot they use instead of a goldfish anyway. It's like a trick.

Yeah, I know but...

Ha, yeah, I know what you're saying.

It's like it's not worth tidying up anyways. Balling up rubbish into a black plastic bin liner. Radio on. Talk radio. A man calls about a problem with his neighbours. Crush a few cans, drop them in the bag. A tree is overhanging his garden, he wants to cut it down. Picking up some crumpled tissue. Can he do that? I mean can he? Jesus Christ. Just cut the thing down man. Lisa is bored. Hanging around. She quits cleaning and sits on the sofa as another call comes through. One time she got offered a job on this new talk radio station. All she'd have to do was sit by the telephone and every once in a while someone from the station would call her up and tell her to phone back and pretend to be somebody else with a question or a point of view that they wanted to get on the air. Anytime their shows were dragging they'd call her or one of the other people they had on the book and she'd get on there with some crackpot view and it'd kick life into the radio show. Paying up forty a call. Only qualification needed was to be able to disguise your voice so it wasn't obvious it was the same few people calling over and over. She hadn't been able to do the voices. She tried out a few. They all either sounded just like her or like some bad club impressionist. Caricatures. Yeah, I had a

<104>

problem with my neighbour too. Jesus. He used to drive stock cars and he'd always be... Lisa turns the dial. Static into symphony music. How long are they going to be? Rattle and a key in the door.

Sitting around. TV on. Loose Joints told Lisa about his kid. Lisa laughed. Ray sat in the kitchen looking at road maps. All of them glancing at the clock thinking about how long they'd got until they had to move. Ray said that they should maybe sleep awhile, that they didn't need to even start moving until 3am. They phoned out for a Chinese, sat watching some film starring Alain Delon, picking at stuff out of tin foil containers. Lisa and Loose Joints smoked a little blow, laughed at the dubbing. Ray smoked a pack. At 3.10 the film ended in a shoot-out. They grabbed their coats and bags, went down the stairs and hit the open road as the first spots of rain spat at the windscreen. Ray fumbled with the knobs on the steering column until he managed to get the wipers going and then lit a cigarette and pushed the button on the door to wind down the window a couple of inches. The rain hammered against the car and Ray had to turn up the stereo so that they could make out the words of the Lightnin' Hopkins tune that was playing.

Lisa fell asleep in the passenger seat. Loose Joints, in the back, was staring out of the window watching the blur of traffic heading back into the city. So this is it then Ray. The last job. You still planning on splitting after this?

Too fucking right I am. Me and Lisa have plans. It's going to be the real deal. Just the two of us, no shit, no worries.

Where are you going to go?

I'm still not sure. Spain I think, maybe Italy. Where would you go?

Loose Joints pulled the band from his hair and shook it out so

<105>

the fringe was like a burnt orange curtain in front of his face. Mount Rushmore he said, as he flicked the hair away from his face.

You're fucking joking, right? What kind of a place is that?

You know the place where they have all those...

Yeah, I know what it is. I mean that's not much of a place to say. You could've said Belize, or Mexico, or even fucking Thailand. I could've seen you there. But Mount Rushmore? What do you want to go there for?

I want to sleep in the nostril of one of those dead presidents.

Ray laughed and looked at Loose Joints who stared back poker faced. He wasn't sure if he was trying to wind him up until Loose Joints' face cracked and he burst out laughing, Yeah, Ray, it's true. I read in a magazine that the nose of one of those carvings was big enough to sleep in and since then, well, that's what I want to do.

Ray pushed the car along, the needle tipping just the right side of seventy all the way. It'd be dumb to pick up a ticket and they had plenty of time. He rapped with Loose Joints about past jobs and their plans for the future then went through their immediate plans for when they arrived in Amsterdam.

They got caught up in a jam with twenty miles to go to the coast and Ray clocked the speed they were moving at less than 10 miles per for the best part of an hour. By the time they reached the port Loose Joints had fallen asleep. When he opened his eyes Ray was putting on the handbrake as he parked up inside the ferry. Lisa was combing her hair, doing up the buttons on her jacket.

You sleep like the fuckin' dead. I thought you would've at least kept awake to talk to me.

Loose Joints stretched out his arms and yawned, Yeah, Ray, sorry. I got caught up counting cones. He looked around him.

<106>

Rust dripping steel. Curving, ridged, beams.

It's like the inside of a rib-cage. We've been swallowed by a dinosaur. I told you man. Ferries are fucking dinosaurs.

<107>

Part Two

Six Inch Bob Dylan
Don't Start Me Talkin'
The Following
Thriving On A Riff
Rudi Calls
American George
Curiosity
Mellomania
Phone Call
More Wrong Than Right
Beauty Contest
The Fish Out Of Water
The Kato Hotel
Dead Meat
The Devilettes
Riddle's Rule
Duplicitous Dialogue
A Lullabye Of Noise
A Night In The Hole
De Schorpioen
Cavemen
Midnight Cold
Harry Waits
The Runaround
The Hot Shot
Red Light
No More Yes
After Hours
Three Past Eight Thirty AM
When The Ocean Meets The Sky
Baby You're Dynamite

<109>

Six Inch Bob Dylan

Bell ringing. Queen Jane grabs Marie by the arm and pulls her clear of the bicycle. Marie gives the guy the finger then sashays on out into the road. Jane catches her up and folds out the map yet again on top of an overflowing rubbish bin. Spreads it out. Jabs a finger at it. Oh God. Where is this place? Didn't we just come this way?

Marie leaned against a shop window. Lit another cigarette. She was wearing black leather jeans and a lime green teeshirt with dayglo yellow lettering spelling out PINKER across the breast. When she took the teeshirt out of the suitcase in the hotel room earlier and put it on Jane screamed, Ohmigod! what is that abomination, and then pleaded with her not to wear it, saying it clashed with her hair, it clashed with her lipstick, it clashed with absolutely everything she could think of and probably a whole lot of stuff that she couldn't. Now Marie wished she hadn't worn it. Not for any of those reasons. Just that it was colder than she'd thought and now her arms were coming up in goose bumps. She looked at her reflection in the shop window, figured that she was looking pretty good anyway and played out a little scene with her cigarette like some romantic heroine while she talked over her shoulder at Jane.

How should I know? This is all starting to look the same to me. One fucking bridge after another. I think we passed this shop here about ten minutes ago. I'm not sure. You got the directions off him. I mean come on. Let's get a cab or at least ask somebody.

Jane folded up the map and took a look around, looking for the street name. She saw a sign, tried to read it, couldn't pronounce it, got the map out again and tried to match the letters with some place on the map.

Marie called her over to look in the shop window. Rocket

<110>

ships, model aeroplanes, flying saucers suspended with nylon line flying over groups of Barbie dolls having picnics, fighting, dancing, riding horses. Marie pointed over to a display case in the corner. Row after row of toys and dolls, all lined up and wrapped in polythene bags like they were being suffocated. Spin-off figures from television shows, cartoons, sci-fi and horror movies. Jane and Marie tried to recognise them, picked out a Kojak, a couple of different Doctor Whos, Hutch but no Starsky, a whole heap of Star Wars stuff, the Lone Ranger, Captain Kirk, Pee Wee Herman. It started them up talking on old TV shows. Jane wanted to know whether Kirk actually fucked all those alien women he picked up every week. Marie said that maybe he did, it depended on whether they could get him out of his corset and then Jane said no way, he didn't even wear a corset and Marie just laughed and made a dig about his barrel chest.

I mean. Wouldn't it be just so cool to have a doll made that looked like you? If you were a movie star. That would be something. Imagine.

Jane and Marie were inside the shop looking at the shelves of toys. Marie reached down a Zorro doll and asked the price then put it back quickly. Then she saw it.

Oh Jane look at this! I have to have it. Marie passed Jane a small figure in a plastic bag. Oh I've just got to have it. Look he's even got little sunglasses on. Come on. It's beautiful. I don't care how much it is. Let's get it.

Jane asked the shop assistant how much the doll was, then wrote a traveller's cheque to cover it. She picked up the doll and handed it over to Marie. Then she got out the map and asked the assistant for directions. They walked out of the shop and took a left and Marie kissed Jane and then she kissed her six inch Bob Dylan.

<111>

Don't Start Me Talkin'

A livid sea, the colour of a four day bruise, rose and fell as Ray and Loose Joints lounged on the green vinyl seats of the ferry's main bar. Ray kicked his heels up onto the table in front of them crushing a silver foil ashtray with his heel. He sipped on a glass of vodka and looked out at the distant shape of a boat on the horizon through the porthole that was behind Loose Joints' shoulder. Lisa was up by the machines slotting in coins, hoping on a hundred jackpot but watching bells, bars and fruit judder to a halt in random patterns.

Loose Joints said he was going out on deck for a while before it started raining again and Ray nodded and said that he'd still be here when he got back and that he didn't know why he was bothering to go out anyway because all there was to see was the fucking sea and couldn't they see the sea from where they were? He watched Loose Joints pick his way through the clusters of chairs and tables and push past a gang of kids that were crowded around a row of video games and acting out the moves on the screen as they waited their turn. If the place hadn't been rocking from side to side, albeit ever so slightly, he could've been in a bar on dry land. With its fruit machines and video jukebox, potted plastic plants and brass fittings, the place had the makings of a West End fun pub.

A group of returning German tourists came and sat at the next table. Cameras hung from fat, rippled necks and they spoke loudly and laughed though Ray couldn't understand what they were saying. One of the group went over and put some money in the video jukebox and the TV that was bracketed above their heads flashed into life. Ray watched Madonna gyrate, grabbing her crotch, pulling open her black jacket to expose her tightly corsetted breasts.

<112>

The video ended and a new song came up. Ray's eyes began to close as the ship gently rocked him to sleep.

When Loose Joints started fanning his face, he woke. Through low-lidded eyes he could make out the money in Loose Joints' hand and for a second or two he thought that he'd somehow sleep-walked through the whole thing and that they were back in London passing out the spoils. He remembered how before he used to get so involved in his work that when it was over, when he'd reached safety, he couldn't remember exactly what had gone on. It was like he'd been riding a train and had disappeared into a long, black tunnel and, when he reached the outside, that part of the journey was a mystery. On his way in it was clear, same when he came out. And in the middle? As he snapped awake, he felt the floor roll underneath him, he heard the Germans laughing at the next table and he saw Loose Joints waving the handful of notes in his face. This train had barely moved out of the station.

Uh, alright how's it going? Sorry it must've been my turn to nod off. Ray mumbled, fumbling a cigarette into his mouth, Where've you been? Where did you get that from?

Loose Joints spread the money out onto the table. I met some guys and played a few hands. Christ, were they drunk?

But you don't play cards.

Ha, well I play a little. I've been studying. But more than that I'm an excellent cheat. Why don't I go and buy us some duty free for when we arrive huh? How much longer are we going to be stuck on this tub?

Ray looked at his watch and made a quick calculation, then he told Loose Joints he may as well settle down because they had an hour or so left yet.

Lisa came over and sat down next to Ray and grabbed his hand.

I saw you sleeping so I thought I'd leave you alone. How are you feeling?

<113>

I'm feeling pretty good, I think. Loose Joints just won a bundle playing cards. How did it go with the machines?

Lisa pulled the insides out of her jeans pockets to show they were empty and then held her palms out.

I've just been up on the deck. Looking out at the sea. You know I like the fact that you can't see land. I like the fact that you're looking out at this mass and it could go on for ever to the edge of the world but I'm there and I'm thinking, this isn't pretty, it's not beautiful, it's just desolate. The only thing that makes the sea pretty is when it touches the land. There's something kind of desperate and sad about waves breaking out here and never hitting a beach.

But they do. They start way out and then...

Yeah. I know that. I know the physics of the thing. I guess I'm not explaining myself very well. It just made me feel sad. That's all. Kind of hopeless.

When Loose Joints returned from the duty free shop, he placed a plastic bag decorated with the logo of a cigarette company on the table and pulled out a bottle of Black Bush and peeled the cellophane from around its neck. He took a long pull, coughed a little, then offered the bottle to Ray who waved it away. Lisa poured a little measure into an empty glass on the table.

Loose Joints lifted another bottle out from the bag, showing Ray the blue label of an expensive bottle of vodka but Ray declined saying that he had to stay alert now, that he couldn't afford to make any errors and that the last thing he wanted was to be pulled over for drink driving and banged up for a day or so at some foreign station and miss the deadline for the delivery.

Yeah, okay Ray I got you. Loose Joints put the bag down but kept hold of the bottle of Bushmills. Do you think we ought to go check on the fish?

Ray shook his head.

It'll be alright, I told you. Don't worry about it. So, tell me how

<114>

you did it? Whether you're a cheat or not you must've had some luck to take that much money at cards in the time I was asleep.

Loose Joints leaned back in his seat and puffed out his chest. Ray, I told you before, I come from a long line of lucky bastards. You make your luck. You know your...

...Angles, yeah.

That's right. That's fucking right. I know them, so I'm safe. That's my business. Did I ever tell you about my uncle? He didn't have it but he tried. Rather he had it and tried too hard. He tried so hard that he was left without a penny. Lost everything on the horses. But he kept at it and he'd starve himself so that he'd have a little money to bet with.

Ray shuffled in his seat to get more comfortable, he'd been sleeping in an odd position and his legs were all tensed up. Go on then, tell me about him. We've got time to kill.

Well, it's like this. This is some advice to you. You already know this but you might forget it. To do anything you have to be confident that you can do it. Doing the thing is easy, it's having the confidence to start it that's the hard part. Like you and me, when we worked it was easy wasn't it?

Ray nodded.

And the hard part, the part that took ages was getting to the stage when we'd decided to do it. Right? Getting to the point when we had the confidence to go ahead. That's knowing the angles. Know them and you're over 90 per cent there already. If you're worried, if it doesn't seem right, then don't do it. There's always another opportunity around the corner.

Ray closed his eyes again but didn't drift back to sleep. He was listening closely to what Loose Joints was saying.

So, this uncle of mine. He used to play the horses. That was all he did. He didn't work. He didn't need to. So for years it was all okay. He even managed to buy himself a house out of the money. Anyways one day, and I don't know why this happened, nobody

<115>

knew, but one day he woke up and he just knew it had gone. All his confidence had gone. He worried about it a little but he went ahead with the horses and then a losing day, became a losing week. So okay, one week, that was alright. He was working it over the year. Over a year he'd be making money. But the weeks turned into months then into a year and then into the next year and... he lost the house, his car. Had to go and live in this pokey little bedsit, one room, Baby Belling in the corner, dripping tap in the sink, shared bathroom, you know that shit. And, like I said, he started starving himself to get the money for the horses. So one day, it was late in the autumn, there were leaves everywhere, dead leaves all over the street. One day he was down to his last few quid and the rent was due, and the heating was broken and... well you know. So he's walking down the road and he sees this glint of silver in the gutter among the leaves. He goes over to it, thinking it's a fifty pence coin or something, but when he clears the leaves away he finds that it's a pen. A silver ballpoint. There's an inscription on the side and he smooths off the dirt from it so he can read it but it's all worn away and all he can make out is St.......l.i...f...eve. Just those letters. But, and remember he hadn't eaten anything for days, I guess he was kind of delirious, he took the letters as being a sign. So he took the pen with him to the betting shop and he scoured all the papers until he saw this horse that was running that had all of those letters in its name. I think it was called something like St Julian's Fever. So of course, he puts all his money on this horse, writes out the ticket with this pen and the fucking thing comes in at 18-1. Next day he goes down to the bookies and he writes out another slip with the pen and that comes in. Took about another year or so until he was back on top but that pen gave him the confidence and when the confidence came back he couldn't help but keep winning.

Ray opened his eyes and reached for the bottle of whisky. So this pen. It was some kind of gift from the gods huh?

<116>

Lisa smiled, looked at Ray, then looked at Loose Joints. You're trying to tell us this was a magic pen?

Loose Joints leaned forwards as though he was about to divulge some great secret. No, it was a promotional thing: Steel is For Ever. My uncle figured that one out as soon as he got it home and examined it. But that wasn't the point you see. It gave him something. It gave him a chance.

Loose Joints, you know something? You are full of shit.

He laughed. Yeah Lisa, right, but hey what better way to pass the time?

<117>

The Following

Rudi, yeah it's me, Harry. We're just about ready to leave. No, no he's here with me. What, you want to speak to him? I'll get him, hang on a minute. Rootboy, hey, over here... No. Okay. Okay. Yeah, the plane leaves in 15 minutes. We've checked in. I just wanted to check on the arrangements. I want to make sure I've got them right, don't I? I call your man then we go straight to Ray's hotel. Then we just wait around until he makes a move. If he heads anywhere other than the American we follow him and I'm to call you straight away. Right?... Yeah, you can trust us. He's here now, you want a word? No, okay, yeah, I've got that. Speak to you later. Yeah, later.

Harry hung up the phone and picked up his briefcase. He turned to Rootboy. Leaning against a pillar dressed in a light blue suit and flowered Hawaiian style shirt, Rootboy was peering over the top of a pair of round mirrored shades at a couple of tanned girls that were pushing a trolley of suitcases across the polished marbled floor.

Take those fuckin' glasses off man. We're indoors and it's raining outside anyway. You look like a fuckin' jerk.

Rootboy sheepishly took off the glasses and hung them from the pocket of his jacket. I thought Rudi wanted to speak to me.

No, he just wanted to make sure I hadn't lost you. Not that there's much chance of it in that get up anyway. What do you think this is? Miami fucking Vice. It looks like you threw up on your shirt.

Look, I've never done this kinda shit before. How am I supposed to know? I think I'm looking the business man. Fucking top.

Harry raised his eyes and looked up at the ceiling and the rows of fluorescent lights that hung there. Okay, okay

<118>

whatever you think.

The stewardess showed them to their seats and Rootboy slipped out of his jacket, exposing to Harry the full horror of his multi-coloured shirt. We're not going to fuckin' Barbados you know. We're supposed to look inconspicuous.

Rootboy, pretending not to hear him, pulled out the information card from the pocket in front of his seat and studied the safety drills as the stewardess acted them out.

The plane began to taxi along the runway and Rootboy leaned back in his seat and gripped the armrests. You know Harry, I think I'm a little nervous. First time I ever took a flight man. First time.

Jesus! Harry shook his head. It's just like a fun-fair ride or something. Like a roller-coaster. What the fuck are you worried about? It'll all be over in an hour.

The plane turned and began to gather speed. Rootboy watched the lights blur outside the window and felt himself pushed back into the seat as the nose of the plane lifted. He closed his eyes and listened to the roar of the engine, then opened them as Harry hissed into his ear.

Jesus man, will you let go of my fuckin' hand.

<119>

Thriving On A Riff

> **Todd Munro reporting:** An intruder broke into an
> importer's store and poured chlorine powder into large
> aquariums, killing $30,000 (£20,000) worth of exotic
> fish from Africa. Some of them jumped out of the
> tanks, said Terry Elder, owner of Aquatic Exotica Inc,
> who suspects that an envious competitor sabotaged his
> business.

Shit. Someone else who takes fish seriously. Lisa folded up the
newspaper and set it down on the floor in the front of the car. Ray
was driving, moving it down the ramp towards the customs
officers. Loose Joints had already split to go through as a foot
passenger. No point in taking a single chance.

Ray steered the car towards the queue of vehicles in the green
channel and drove on in second gear. Two uniformed men
stepped out of a small illuminated kiosk and gestured that he
should stop. Ray pulled over, switched off the engine and opened
his window. A honey coloured alsatian was pacing up and down
on a long leash that one of the officers held wrapped around his
clenched fist.

What is your destination? The man spoke with a heavy accent,
French, but reminding Ray of a Nazi officer in any of a hundred
matinees.

Amsterdam.

The man leaned an arm on the roof of the car and pushed his
head through the window so he could see into the back of the car.
Have you anything to declare?

Ray and Lisa shook their heads simultaneously and Ray said
no, while Lisa mumbled a quote from Wilde. Ray gave her a
quick dig in the ribs with his elbow. He could see the handle of a

<120>

regulation issue police hand gun, holstered and hanging at eye level as the man leaned against the car door.

The man continued to stare into the car and the other officer was leading the dog around the back of the car. In the wing mirror Ray saw the animal sniffing around the rear tyre.

There was a bang on the roof and one of the customs officers barked at Ray to get moving. He started up the engine and eased the car back onto the roadway, accelerating gently until he'd reached a bend in the road and the border guards had disappeared from view.

Loose Joints saw them coming and stuck out his thumb. He'd hustled his way through to the front of the queue, got through double quick and had been hanging around by the roadside for a quarter hour.

Lisa leaned over and opened the back door to let him in.

Any trouble?

No trouble at all.

The route had been written out for Ray, all the major roads were noted in blue ink, in hesitant block capitals. Lisa held the directions as they pushed on through sleepy French streets and on towards the autoroute. Loose Joints worked on the last of the Bushmills.

If you hadn't drunk so much you could've taken over for a while.

Loose Joints capped the bottle. Well, I'm more than ready anyway. Anytime you want.

Ray glanced over at him in the rear view mirror. Saw Loose Joints smiling drunkenly, slouched in the back seat. You have got to be fucking joking.

Hey Ray! Lisa shouted. Grabbed his arm.

What?

<121>

Right side. Right side. Right fucking side!! Lisa grabbed the wheel and turned it quickly. A flash of headlights passed them close up on the left. The car's horn faded.

Shit Ray, pay attention. Right side of the road. Are you sure you don't want me to take over?

Ray muttered something under his breath gripping the wheel tightly in both hands and staring straight ahead at the white line that curved away into the distance.

No way, just stay awake and tell me when to turn.

Rain came down. Dark clouds. Morning but it could have been dusk. Ray flicked on the lights. Rain swept the roads, caught in the yellow beams like scratches on old film prints. Ray fought the gloom with bleary white eyes and fists wrapped around the laced leatherette of the steering wheel. Driving like this was like falling in a dream, endless, only the feeling of movement without any means of gauging it. Ray forced his eyes open, forced the car on, concentrated on the white line. It wasn't that he was even tired. It was more that he was concentrating so much, on so much, that he was barely able to focus. The road unravelled like a video game.

We hang a right in a minute, then it's about five miles to the autoroute. It looks pretty simple from there. Loose Joints had the directions opened out on the back seat.

Okay. Look out for the sign. If you can see anything in this fucking rain. And either tune the fucking radio in or stick on a tape.

Lisa grabbed a cassette from a bag in the glove-box and slotted it in. Ray started tapping out the rhythm on the dash and shouting good choice and blow man blow! When Loose Joints threw him a bemused look he explained that he'd always wanted to shout that while hauling distance along strange open roads.

<122>

Rudi Calls

Okay. It's on its way. Safe assured. And your stuff to me?... Well I need it yesterday, it's running down... Get somebody else. It can't be that difficult... You do? Good... No. I don't need to know about that. You can call later... Now listen, you stupid fuck. This new stuff is certain. Guaranteed. You'll see... No. No. No. We had a guy from California working on the preliminaries. It'll clean up. It's different... No, not that different. Just enough... Well that's it, isn't it? I have the expertise and you have the facilities. We're moving up. We're ahead of the game on this one... Yeah, I heard about that and I stamped it out... We had him skinned. Literally. They found him on the floor all peeled and his skin bunched up in the corner like dirty laundry... Of course. It's not that difficult... No. I'm not joking. Do I joke? Huh, do I make jokes about business? Ask that friend of yours... Well you've got to *hand* it to him... Yeah, that was a joke... So look. It'll be there soon. Take it. Work on it then get back to me... No. I'll give you days. Weeks? What kind of arsehole do you think you're dealing with? Weeks? Fuck. Days is all you'll need... Technical support is available. Of course it is... Are you a complete idiot? Are you pulling my string? If I sent him out first then I may as well have sent you the recipe and you could've been up and running... Fuck, you wouldn't try and rip me off. Like fuck. This way I don't even give you the chance... Yeah, I know it's a big investment. But that's the way it is. You want to play, you got to put up a stake... I know. That's why I took it to you. You're the best there is. That's why I'm giving you the sample... Oh bullshit. Man I can feel your fingers on my dick from here. Don't try jerking me around. I don't need it and I don't fucking want it. We're square here. You'll be receiving soon. I have a messenger on the way. End of story... No you don't know him.

<123>

He'll call you... Of course you can trust him. He needs to do it. He doesn't even know what he's got... Yes. You don't need to know anything about that... Yes. I have some people taking care of that. You met one of them already... Yeah, the guy that's visited you before... No. That wouldn't be smart, would it? There's a risk. When there's a risk I play a pawn... A mule. Yes. Certainly. But I have it covered... I told you. Guaranteed... That's all there is... Yeah, call me. I'm waiting.

<124>

American George

A framed Paul Klee print on the wall. *Dance of the Red Skirts* written on a paper sticker stuck at the bottom of the frame. A huge mirror. White leather sofa. Two wicker armchairs stuffed with cream and brown scatter cushions, owls embroidered on them with pieces of mirror sewn on as eyes. A big window with venetian blinds drawn. Sunlight slipping, sliding through the slats. A low black coffee table on top of which are scattered some glossy magazines. In the corner a metal litter bin, partially hidden by the drooping leaves of an over watered dragon tree. A pair of matt black speakers on brackets in the corner murmur some light guitar music, soft like Bonifa magic. An open door leading to the landing and two flights of steps down to the street. Another black door with a peephole two thirds of the way up. A keyhole but no handle on the outside. Resolutely closed. Queen Jane Approximately and Absolutely Sweet Marie staring at the closed door. Watch a fly crawl across it, take off, buzz around the paper lightshade hanging from the ceiling.

Jane looks at her watch again then turns to Marie, speaking in a whisper.

How long have we been waiting now? Are we too early or something?

No we got here at the right time. I know. I checked the time you wrote down before we left. He should be out soon. He said he was only going to be a few minutes.

Maybe he's waiting to see if we lose our nerve. He's probably spying on us through the peephole right now.

Jane lit a cigarette then started looking for an ashtray. She couldn't find one and went over to the plant pot to stub it out in the damp soil just as the door opened. A man with a yellow moustache stepped out.

<125>

Sorry to keep you. I had some important business to attend to. So, you want to be in the movies. Come inside and we'll talk.

Marie smiled and got up off the sofa, Jane walked over and held out her hand. The man took it and led her through into the next room. Marie followed.

The man motioned for them to sit on a pair of chrome and black plastic chairs in front of the desk. He sat behind it, shuffled some papers, dropped them into an open drawer and leaned his elbows on the desk.

Okay. So which of you is Jane?

Jane nodded mutely.

Right. So you must be Marie? I'm right? My name is American George. Now Jane, I understand that you spoke to my partner on the telephone and he has outlined the kind of pictures that we make.

Yes. Well we're under no illusions if that's what you mean.

George smiled and continued. Well the films we make, and, if I say so myself, the films that have made our name internationally respected and admired, are what we call erotic escapism. Call it porn if you like, but we find that a little euphemism here and there makes it all run so much more smoothly. We expect you to work hard and we expect professionalism.

Marie shifted on her chair, looked at Jane who was sitting quietly with her hands on her lap like she was in a headmaster's office, then looked sternly at George. She examined his suit, the collar of his shirt, noticed the neatness of the knot in his tie, the green stone in the gold ring on the little finger of his left hand, the white handkerchief poking out of his breast pocket. Gold and mother of pearl cufflinks. Sitting behind the desk. Confident. Neatly combed blond hair, trimmed moustache. Blue eyes. He looked like money. Like he was probably worth going along with.

So she said: George. Save it. We are here to earn some money. Jane appears to be under some misguided notion that you are

<126>

going to make her a star. Regardless of whether that happens or doesn't happen, the bottom line is that we are here because you are going to pay us to act out some scenes in a porn film and all that you have to tell us is what you want us to do, where you want us to go, when you want us to be there and, most importantly, how much you're going to pay us when we've done it.

George leaned back in his chair, a huge grin cracked over his face. Right. Let's talk business then. We require two special ladies for a particular feature that will start shooting shortly. I think that the pair of you may be perfectly suited. Obviously I will need to see some proof of that. As you have been so direct with me, I'll be direct with you. Take off your clothes.

Marie stood up. She peeled off her lime green teeshirt, exposing small, rounded breasts. She unfastened the buckle of her belt, unzipped her leather jeans and pulled them down. Jane watched her, then stood up and started to undress.

They stood naked in the centre of the office. George came over and began to examine them: Jane's breasts, the big, pink nipples, then down at her crotch and the tiny dick poking out of a dark nest of pubic hair. Then Marie. Shaved. White skin smooth. He sat on the edge of the desk.

Perfect. Now can you get those things hard?

Jane nodded.

What about you? It's important. That's why we're prepared to pay so much. We need them hard. I know how it is. I'm sympathetic. But I can assure you it is absolutely essential for this project. It's easy getting beautiful girls. It's easy getting good looking guys. But if you try and get something in between... Well it's not so easy. Ugly old she-males we don't need. That's not the kick we're trying to give. We need lookers who are... well let's just say... versatile. We get them in here, looking fine and then we get on set... I don't know if it's because they're pumped so full of

<127>

hormones or just plain stage fright but if you can't get a hard-on and shoot good... A Hollywood loaf's nothing. No dice. Just no dice at all.

Marie nodded. Grabbed her dick, started stroking it, pulling on it until it started to swell.

George walked around the desk, sat back down in his chair.

Both of you. I do need to see that they're working.

Jane grasped her cock and massaged it. She felt it grow in her hand. She glanced over at Marie who was moaning a little, the veins starting to show, blood pumping and she stroked a little faster. She'd never fucked Marie. Had never even thought about it. They were close, sure. But it was love like sisters. Now she was getting turned on by watching Marie masturbate in front of a man that they'd only just met. She pumped a little harder, gasped, then came over her hand. A little spurt and a dribble of come on her knuckles, trickling over the snake ring. Marie worked harder. Breathing heavily. Biting on her bottom lip until she too ejaculated. Shudder. And she grasped a chair for support.

Fantastic. Excellent. George clapped his hands. Perfect. I can see why Harry gave you such a good report. You've got it Jane, really, we can make something here. Now get dressed and leave your hotel name and room number with me and I'll get back to you.

Marie wiped off on a tissue from the box of Kleenex that George had handed to her, passed the box to Jane. She stepped into her jeans, pulled on her teeshirt.

Look George. We're not in the habit of putting on free shows. We expect a little more from you than a vague promise of a phonecall, so take your hand from your hard-on under that desk and give us the real deal.

Jane finished dressing and went over and stood by Marie.

George rocked back on his chair. Right. I like your attitude. You ask and I'll tell you. I'll give you the parts. You look good.

<128>

You look perfect. I don't give a shit if you can act. The film starts shooting at the end of the month. It's pretty straightforward. Girl on girl. Man on girl. Foursomes. Threesomes. Sevensomes. You get the picture. Anything goes except animals and children. I won't bullshit you, we do make those kind of films. This just isn't one of them. You're okay with that? George didn't give them time to answer, just carried on like he was talking to an empty room, like he was reading out the same lines for the hundredth time... I'm talking CP, SM, BD. Jane gets the lead. Because, let's face it Marie, she's better looking. I dig the shaved bit though. Keep that.

Jane stifled a smile and asked if she was going to get her picture in the publicity photos like she'd been told and American George said that he'd be mad to do otherwise. Marie said, Well this is all fine but I want to hear the figures. How much are we talking about here?

George tapped out some digits on a calculator that he'd pulled from the desk drawer. He frowned then pressed a couple more buttons. This is how it runs. Marie, you get a flat two thousand, that's sterling. Jane picks up three plus one point on net profits as the star. This is for a three day shoot. It's a big production. You won't find better.

You said that the filming doesn't start until the end of the month. What are we expected to do until then?

I don't know. It's up to you. If you need money to hang around until shooting starts then I'm afraid I can't offer any advances but I can probably sort you out with a little work to tide you over. Talk about it, then call me back. I'll have the contracts drawn up later today and they'll be ready to sign tomorrow. Just leave your full names on this pad on your way out. And I mean your real names. You realise this is an exceptional deal we're offering. Truly exceptional. And I think you'll prove to me that you're worth it.

American George pushed a lined A4 pad across the desk then picked up the telephone and tapped out a number. Queen Jane

<129>

Approximately and Absolutely Sweet Marie wrote their names on the pad and waited. American George started talking in Dutch on the telephone, waving them out of the room without even looking up. They made their way out and down the stairs with Marie muttering that she didn't trust the jerk, that she thought they were being stiffed and that for all the chance they had of making money out of something as skewed as this then they may as well just go home. Jane pointed out that they'd come this far and what did they have to lose by sticking around. Marie thought about it, shrugged and suggested that they go and get something to eat.

<130>

Curiosity

They'd dropped off Loose Joints near Dam square. Watched him disappear into the crowd, wandering off, looking for a hotel. After taking an age to find a space, Ray had parked up a few streets away from the hotel marked on the map by Rudi. A reservation made in the name of Mr and Mrs John Burrows had secured them a spacious double ensuite room right at the top of the building. Now Ray was stretched out on the bed, his arms behind his head staring at the sealed black jar that stood on the dresser. Lisa lay in a steaming bath with her eyes closed.

Ray, don't you think you should give that number a call?

Yeah, in a minute baby. I think I'll just lay around here for a while first. We've got plenty.

Lisa got out of the bath, wrapped a towel around her wet hair and walked into the room, dripping wet. She flicked her fingers at Ray, splashed water on him. She lay down on the bed next to him, wrapped her arm around his waist. When will we hear from Loose Joints?

Ray sat up, pulled the towel from Lisa's head and started to massage her hair dry. He kissed the back of her neck. Well, after he's got himself a room he's going to call up the guy he knows and see if he can arrange a meeting for me. When he's done that he'll come here and let us know what's going on. I'll deliver the fish later today and I guess you're going to have to wait here until he comes. I can't see it taking me very long.

Do you think we should have a look at the thing? Make sure it's alright.

No. Rudi said to leave it alone. It's bound to be alright.

But what happens if they open it up and the poor thing's floating belly up in the jar?

No. It'll be alright. I think we should leave it alone. Let's just

<131>

get rid of it. I'll go and call now. Ray slipped on his jacket and checked the pocket for the envelope with the contact number in it. I'll go and make the call from a payphone. It won't take a minute.

Lisa listened to Ray's footsteps disappearing down the corridor then walked over to the window and pulled back the net curtain. She watched a tram slide along the street in front of the hotel. On either side she could see a canal, a glass-roofed boat moving along. She saw Ray cross the street and walk past a bar with palm trees and pink flamingos painted on its windows and her eyes followed him as he walked over the canal bridge, stopping for a moment to watch another boat, a canal taxi, pass underneath him then continue on out of sight.

Lisa went over to the dresser and picked up the jar. She dug her fingernails into the seal at the top and then, ever-so-carefully, began to peel the top layer of rubber away.

<132>

Mellomania

Harry craned his neck and banged his head against the glass of the bar window.

Did he have it with him?

He rubbed his head and settled back in his seat. I'm not sure. I don't think so. All these birds and trees painted on the window I couldn't see shit.

So, do we follow him now or what?

No. She must still be in the hotel there. I can't see him going far without her. Let's just sit tight and relax.

Harry opened up a small plastic bag of grass and started rolling a joint. Rootboy went and ordered another couple of Heineken. Harry lit up and the joint popped and hissed in his fingers as he took a long pull. They passed it between them and looked out of the window. Rootboy started laughing, slipped on his shades muttering, Cool. This is a fucking cool stakeout.

<133>

Phone Call

Ray stepped into a green phone booth and took the envelope from his pocket. He laid out the paper with the number on it and dropped in some change. He pressed the receiver to his ear and plugged his other ear with his thumb as a tram rattled by. After a moment of silence the call was connected, on the the third ring it was answered.

Hello Ray.

He didn't recognise the voice. The English was perfect, only a slight hint of an accent.

I have been expecting your call. Do you have the fish?

Yes. I have it. It's safe.

Excellent. Now could you bring it to me as soon as possible. I'll give you the address. From where you are you should be able to get to me within the hour. We'll meet at the American Hotel, 97 Liedsekade. I'll spell it out for you. L-I-E-D... Actually why don't you just take a cab? Ask for the American Hotel. I'm looking forward to meeting you.

Ray opened his mouth to speak but the phone line was dead. He backed out of the booth and headed back to the hotel.

<134>

More Wrong Than Right

First Loose Joints called home, talked to the kid about the big boat and the weather and said that he'd pick him up something nice as a present and bring it home in a couple of days. Then he called his man and told him that he was in town and that his friend was itching to meet him about making the run. He explained how he was merely acting as the go-between and that his role in the deal, should it come off, was strictly passive. A manager's cut if you like, pick up a percentage at the end of the show. Loose Joints' man said that he thought all of this sounded fine and if LJ was prepared to put forward this guy then he must be a straight up, regular guy and why didn't he just tell his friend to come along to a bar called De Schorpioen where there would be someone to meet him until midnight and if LJ didn't want to go, then that was alright with him after all but why didn't he come and meet them in their club for a drink later on anyway and make use of the facilities? His name would be on the door. It would be a shame not to at least have a drink together after he'd come all this way. Loose Joints said he might just do that and that that sounded a fine way to pass some time.

Loose Joints lay back down on his hotel bed and turned on the TV with the remote. He flicked through a few channels until he hit on a cartoon. Foghorn Leghorn. Dubbed into German. Loose Joints laughed at the screen as the rooster tried to get the guard dog with one dirty trick after another. After the bird came a Roadrunner double and Loose Joints noticed that although there weren't any words, somebody had dubbed a laugh track over the cartoon. He sat there watching the show, hearing the laughter and wondered whether they took the sound from some other film or whether they hired people, took them into a studio and got them to laugh on cue into a microphone. He picked up on one

<135>

particular laugh, high like a horse or something, that seemed to go on for slightly longer than the rest of them. Then he noticed that this particular laugh always came in the same place so he figured that it must just be the same set of laughter dubbed on over and over. By the time he'd finished thinking about this he realised that the cartoons were finished and, even though Roadrunner, and specifically Wile E Coyote was his favourite cartoon character, he hadn't laughed once. This seemed to him to be yet another example of why it didn't do so well to go around analysing every thing you saw or read right up the arsehole. That some things are better just to take on face value. If you find it funny just laugh, or if something scares you then be scared, don't go looking stop-frame for the latex under the fake blood.

Only thing was he couldn't do it. He always needed to know the trick, how the mirrors pulled off magic. It was what gave him an edge. In real time you were always playing against an unfavourable percentage. More things were able to go wrong than right. So what you needed to do was to find out how many things had gone wrong already, and in what order and that gave you enough information to increase your percentages. Like a case down player at Blackjack, not something that Loose Joints had ever attempted to do professionally but something he'd been studying with a view to maybe moving in that direction a little later on. Just keep counting the cards. In the end you're still going to lose with the same certainty that one day you're going to die. It's just a matter of trying to win more than you lose or at least try for evens and then you're letting death creep up on you slowly instead of hurtling at you like a steam train 100 miles per.

Loose Joints had been thinking about Ray and Lisa and Rudi and the fish. It had seemed a little screwed to begin with but the more he thought about it the less he liked it. This was why he'd been keeping his distance from the whole deal, why he'd insisted on staying in a separate hotel and why he was planning to go

<136>

back to London on his own. In fact, if he'd known the man wasn't going to insist on a personal introduction to Ray then he could've managed without coming along at all. He walked over to the night-table and picked up the phone and started tapping in Ray's hotel number.

<137>

Beauty Contest

Marie had been to Venice and Venice stank. Oh alright it might look beautiful and everything. Canals and little boats and little bridges but it still stank. Fetid green water. Like the blocked drain outside the kitchen window of her old flat in Archway. As beautiful as that. She watched a boat cruise by, heard the commentary fade away and looked over to Jane who was reading a ripped red vinyl menu and sucking on a cigarette. Joni Mitchell's *Big Yellow Taxi* dripping out of the speaker above the cafe door wasn't helping Marie's mood. The canals stank like ditches here too.

She couldn't quite put her finger on why she was feeling so depressed. She was sure it couldn't have been just because American George had said that she wasn't as good looking as Jane. I mean it's not as if he'd said that she was ugly or anything. Anyway it wasn't a beauty contest. And George himself. Although he was obviously a loathsome piece of shit she had met worse. That didn't matter. Jane had her heart set on this. Maybe the film could be fun. Fuck it. Let it roll.

The waiter came over with his pad and his pencil and asked if they were ready to order. Marie looked at the tattoos on his forearms. Vibrant colours, azure and crimson. A bird of paradise with long bright tail feathers stretching up and around the bicep. A unicorn with a flowing mane. Marie had a tattoo. Up high on her shoulder. A tiny flower. It was supposed to be a rose but it was so ineptly done that it looked more like a birthmark. Still, she'd seen worse. One of the doormen at the last club she'd worked at had his fingers tattooed. L-O-V-E on his right hand. H-A-T on his left hand. Love and hat. The E was missing. No letter just a blue dot like a full stop. He'd done the lettering himself when he was drunk and had passed out before he could finish any more than

<138>

the first prick on the little finger of his left hand. People had started calling him The Hat and he thought that was cool so he never bothered with the E. He just left it. He wasn't very bright.

<139>

The Fish Out of Water

Ray came running up the stairs, opened the door and came into the room calling to Lisa. He got half-way through saying that he'd fixed up the drop and that they were near finished with the fish at last when he saw Lisa holding up the jar in the middle of the room. He could see right through it. The covering was all peeled away and he saw shards of thick black rubber scattered over the floor. He could see right through it, through the glass, through the liquid right through to the window and the sky that reflected, all curved and distorted through the jar.

He could see it all but he couldn't see any fish.

Shit. Where is it?

It's not here Ray.

What? What do you mean not here? It couldn't hardly have escaped by itself could it? I mean Jesus Christ, it couldn't have just vanished. When did you open it up? Why?

No Ray. You don't understand. There isn't a fish. I don't think there ever was one. Did you see it? I mean when he gave you the jar did you see a fish in it?

Well no. It was all sealed up. You saw that. That's how he gave it to me.

All I know is that I peeled some of the rubber away, just a little bit, and I looked in and I couldn't see anything. So I peeled off a bit more. I only wanted to make sure the thing was still alive. Look, you can see there's nothing in here. The top of the jar is still sealed. I haven't opened it. I don't think there ever was anything in it other than this water.

Ray sat on the edge of the bed, picked up a piece of the rubber covering from the carpet and rolled it between his fingers. He asked Lisa to pass him the jar and he held it up to the light and swirled the contents around inside. Close up he could see that the

<140>

liquid had a slight bluish tint.

I don't understand it Ray. Why would Rudi go to so much trouble to get a jar of water brought over here? It doesn't make any sense.

I don't think this is water. You'd front somebody a grand in cash to set up some stupid fucking joke or something?

Ray put the jar back down on the table and lit a cigarette. He started pacing around the room, all the time staring at the jar. He couldn't figure it out. Then he started onto thinking about this guy he used to know who set up a little laboratory in his garage. All pipes and tubes and blue-flamed Bunsen burners and how he'd shown Ray how he could manufacture all kinds of stuff and how you took some sheets of blotting paper and you soaked them in this liquid and then you got a crazy design printed in tiny squares on them and then you had...

He froze. Stared at the jar then blurted out, That's it. It must be. That fucker.

Lisa looked puzzled. What is it? What do you mean? Ray. Ray?

He grabbed the jar and held it up in front of them both. It's some kind of drug. Something in liquid form...

Do they make drugs like that?

Yeah of course. If you're making acid blotters then you soak sheets of paper in a liquid containing LSD. That would make some kind of sense. We don't have the time to test it out and I don't think I'd want to either but my guess is that the stuff in that jar is a drug of some description. Certain.

But this is Amsterdam. Surely there's enough stuff here already without having to bring in more? Shit Ray, whoever heard of smuggling drugs from England into Amsterdam? You'd have to be crazy. It's not worth the risk.

Yeah, but Rudi didn't take any risks did he? We did. But I get what you're saying. There has to be something more to this. Rudi went to a lot of trouble over this jar and he's either some seriously

<141>

sick practical joker or this is worth a lot to him. I'm going to lay odds on the second.

Okay. But what do we do now? Are you going ahead with taking the jar to the guy or what?

Ray was going around the room taking their stuff out of their bags. He hung a shirt in the wardrobe, laid a couple of teeshirts on the back of the chair. He zipped up one of the bags then started taking things out of the other.

No. First thing we do is check out of here. Rudi got us this room and it's possible that he's got somebody watching us right now. We'll get another place to stay. Then I call Rudi and see what he has to say about this. For now just get together anything you think you'll actually need and leave the rest here. Make it look like someone is using the room. If I don't show at the American Hotel within an hour they'll know something's going on and the first place they'll try is here.

Why don't we just split? We could go back.

No. Definitely not. If it turns out we're holding a large jar of some hot shit and the opportunity arises to turn that substance into money, then there's no place I'd rather be than right here. Plus, don't forget, I have the deal with Loose Joints to set up. This could all work out exactly right. He kissed Lisa and urged her to hurry up with her stuff.

In five minutes they had the place looking like they'd been staying there a fortnight. Ray turned on the TV, adjusted the volume so it was loud enough to be heard through a closed door but not loud enough to warrant any complaints from the neighbouring rooms. They were just on their way out of the door when the phone on the table by the bed started ringing, a red light flashing on top of it every time it sounded. Lisa looked at Ray and asked if he was going to answer it and he checked his watch and worked out that it'd been just a quarter hour since he'd put the phone down on the guy at the hotel so it was unlikely to be him

<142>

and that anyway, it would be more suspicious if he didn't answer it.

He walked over and picked it up and found Loose Joints on the other end saying Ray, I'm getting a bad feeling on this. And Ray saying you and me both and explaining to Loose Joints about the jar and asking what did he think about that? Loose Joints thought it over a second and then said to Ray that he was probably right or maybe he was wrong or... How the fuck could he say? You do your thing Ray. Play it like you would anyway. And, just supposing that he was right in his assumption, then what he would do would be to phone Rudi and to try and bluff him in to giving him the gen on the jar and then hold the thing to ransom for some more money and if Rudi wouldn't go for that then to try and offload it somewhere else. That was if it was what they thought it was and if it wasn't, then when Ray called up he could expect Rudi to be laughing until his balls dropped off and that no one would play a joke past that point so then they'd know for sure. Then Loose Joints gave Ray the address of De Schorpioen bar. I think it means the Scorpion. I guess it must do. Sounds the same. And then said that Ray was to go there anytime before midnight and wait until somebody approached him. Ray asked how this somebody was going to know who he was and wouldn't it be better if Loose Joints came along too and made the introductions? Loose Joints explained that he wasn't needed and he wasn't keen on being involved unnecessarily and that he'd given the man a rough description of Ray in any case. He was sure they'd connect. The Schorpioen was a quiet bar, almost exclusive, if you weren't invited or expected then you most likely wouldn't even get through the door. Then Loose Joints wished Ray all the best and told him not do anything unless he was a hundred per cent that it was the right thing to do. Pointing out that this whole scene was an opportunity, nothing more, and if it all went up in flames then it was better to back off and wait for

<143>

another time rather than try and drag the opportunity out of the fire and get seriously burned. If he found his hands were too full with Rudi and the jar, then to call him back and he'd make excuses for why Ray couldn't show at De Schorpioen. If he needed any advice then Loose Joints would be around town having fun and hanging out for a couple more days and after that he'd be back home where he'd be waiting for Ray to come shower him with banknotes one way or another.

Ray hung up and followed Lisa through the door and they walked quickly down the stairs and into the street. They jumped on the first tram they saw, headed to Centraal Station.

<144>

The Kato Hotel

They'd only been in the railway station a couple of minutes when a young man with a shaved head and a goatee beard approached Lisa. He wore a green army jacket and had his eyebrow and nose pierced with matching silver hoops. He described the hotel he was working for, how busy it was, how cheap it was. Lisa looked at the map on the card the man had given her, saw that hotel was within walking distance and asked if he knew for definite that they had rooms available. The man said that he was sure that they had when he'd left earlier in the day but that the next big international train was due in another half-hour so it would probably be a good idea to get there now. When the international trains came in he would be passing out dozens of these cards and because the place was cheap and easy to reach, its rooms filled up quick. Lisa thanked the man and caught hold of Ray's hand leading him out the main exit of the station in the direction the tout had told them. Pushing past drunks and scruffy, sallow youths weighed down by rucksacks searching for some intoxication in the city streets.

The Kato Hotel was a tall, thin building, brown stone with blue painted shutters on each window. It stood on a dark, narrow street between a dilapidated church and a small supermarket that was closed up for the night, rolling metal grills covering its doors and windows. There was just one room left when Ray and Lisa got there and they checked in under false names and Ray paid the desk clerk up front and told him not to disturb them because they just wanted a quiet night. You know, quiet. Ray winked. He picked up a tourist map from the desk and then they climbed six flights of steep, narrow, uncarpeted stairs to the room at the top of the hotel. It was far smaller than the room in the first hotel. Painted battleship grey with two hard iron beds set against the

<145>

wall. Above each bed was a Van Gogh print each framed in peeling gold covered plastic. A three-quarter size freestanding wardrobe was against one wall. Opposite, under the tiny barred window, was a wooden table, on it an empty bottle of Perrier water with the label peeled from it and a dead flower drooping from its neck.

They sat down on the rough grey wool blanket at the foot of the bed and Lisa noticed an abandoned spider web spanning the gap from the ceiling to the cable and the bare light bulb. She'd never been in one but the room reminded her of a prison cell. Ray looked at her like he could read her mind and said that yeah, it certainly was like some kind of prison.

So what happens now?

Ray had opened up the map and was looking to see where the bar was located that Loose Joints had told him about.

I'm not sure. Firstly I think we should wait a little while. I'm not certain that somebody didn't follow us from the hotel. It's possible. I'll wait until dark and then call Rudi and see what he has to say. I think they must be missing me by now. I should've dropped off the jar over an hour ago. After that I go and see the guy Loose Joints has set me up with. After that... well I guess we'll just have to see.

You're expecting me to stay here?

I don't see any way else to play it. We'll just be more conspicuous moving around together. I don't know what's going to happen baby. I get the feeling that if we play this right it'll be good. It'll give us the means to do whatever we want. But until I know how the whole thing looks I'd prefer to just put my own skin on the line. You can understand that, can't you?

Lisa nodded and wrapped her arms around Ray, kissed him. I've got good faith in you boy. I think we can make it.

Too fucking right we can make it. This is the gift horse that just coughed up the golden egg. If you see what I'm saying.

<146>

Lisa laughed and said too right she did but that she was still worried, still wondering whether playing off Rudi was a wise thing to be trying.

Ray told her of course it was and almost managed to convince himself. He silently went over it again, he'd go out later, call up Rudi from some public box—the room didn't have a phone and the callbox in the lobby was an open booth right next to the desk. He could wait, letting Rudi get wound up tight before he called and still make it to De Schorpioen before twelve o'clock…

Ray pulled a red Pentel from the zip pocket in the side of Lisa's bag and turned to look at the map. He scanned the index of places of interest, picked out one of the museums and traced the grid references across with his finger, finally marking a little cross onto the map.

Right look. If I'm not back by morning and I haven't got a message to you, don't worry. If I think I'm being followed or I think any odd shit at all is going down then I'm not going to lead them back here. I've marked this place on the map. He tapped at it with the lid of the pen. It's a museum. A little way out from the centre but it should be easy enough to reach and there must be some kind of cafe there. Meet me at ten o'clock. If things get really bad or if I don't show up there, then call up Loose Joints and go back to London with him.

Ray gave the map to Lisa and pointed the place out to her. He didn't like mentioning the possibility of his not being able to make the meeting with her. He didn't like raising any doubts at all but he had to cover every angle. In any case, if he did set up the deal at De Schorpioen and if he could pull something more out of Rudi then he'd been thinking it might not be such a bad idea for Lisa to head back without him. That way she didn't run any risk at all.

Lisa hugged him, pulled him to her, started stroking his hair, kissed him but he broke away saying, Don't worry baby, don't

<147>

worry about a thing. Then he got up, walked over to the window and peered at the sky through the bars.

For the next few hours he watched night descending, saw lights flickering on in streets and buildings across the city. Lisa lay back on the bed and closed her eyes while he smoked his way through eleven cigarettes and hardly said a word.

<148>

Dead Meat

Rudi opened the wooden box on his desk and yanked out a menthol cigarette like he was snapping the rib of a child. He could feel the music from the club below pulsing through the soles of his shoes. A few minutes earlier he'd heard that Ray hadn't shown at the American Hotel and now Harry was on the line spilling more shit on him. He gripped the bakelite phone, squeezing it hard until his fingers were lard white. He lit the cigarette with the jumping butane flame of the pistol cigarette lighter, took a drag and then howled rage down the phone line, smoke spewing out of his mouth like a cartoon explosion.

You are a fucking grade one imbecile. I mean it. You are a fucking worthless, useless, hopeless piece of dogshit and when this is over you can be sure I'm going to wipe you off my heel and flush you down the nearest drain. Guaranteed. Fucking guaranteed. I cannot believe what I'm hearing. The easiest fucking job in the world and you and that laughing clown of a cunt of a big cocked friend of yours have fucked it. Well you're fucked. Do you hear me? I said fucked. Fucking fucked to be exact. FUCKED!...

Harry held the phone away from his ear as Rudi barked a stream of near incomprehensible obscenities down the line. Rootboy stood behind him, stifling a giggle in a dope haze, red eyed, swigging from a bottle of Amstel. Harry waited for a pause in Rudi's tirade, found a second of silence and jumped in. Yeah, Rudi okay. Calm down. It wasn't our fault. We saw them leave the hotel and we followed them. We had to keep our distance. He knows us and he would've made us straight away if we'd got too close. So we were following them and then they jumped on this tram just as it was pulling away and...

Rudi took the knife from his desk drawer and started digging

<149>

it into the wood, splintered it, jabbed the knife in deep. And did you even think to find out where this tram was heading?

Yeah. Of course. It went to the train station. That's where we are now but it's packed, it's steaming with people. I don't think we're going to be able to pick them up. If they even took the tram this far they might've taken a train out of town or anything by now.

Rudi held the tip of the knife to the phone, like he was threatening Harry all down the line, across the land, across the sea. He tapped the point of the blade against the mouthpiece. Calmer now. Spoke slowly through gritted teeth. Don't you think you ought to ask around? See if anybody saw them? You're fucking clueless in any case.

Well we're doing that. We have been. Nothing's turned up yet.

Try fucking harder. Try fucking harder than you've ever tried before because if it ends up that I've got to go there and sort this out myself then the pair of you are going to end up giving each other's severed dicks a blowjob. And if you really can't find anything then get in touch with the guy you met last time I sent you over. That's your last shot. He's into this thing as deep as me and he is not going to be happy with your piss poor performance either.

Rudi slammed down the phone then he reached across the desk and buzzed the intercom. Frank. Get a copy of that picture of Ray that we got on the security camera and fax it over to American George in Amsterdam. Ray must've gotten curious and now he's giving those arsewipes the runaround. Get the picture sent straight away and let them know that if they find him he's fucked. Ray Gardner is dead meat.

<150>

The Devillettes

But Marie, you look absolutely divine. In any case you'll be in that cubicle all night and nobody will see anything more than your head and shoulders. I'm the one that should be complaining.

Well you're going to be behind the bar, aren't you? I mean they can hardly expect you to wait tables here, can they? I think it might give the game away.

Queen Jane Approximately and Absolutely Sweet Marie stood in a tiny graffiti scarred dressing room in the basement of a nightclub called the Bottomless Pit. They were dressed in identical skimpy red costumes with high skirts and low fronts. Each of them had a pair of red plastic devil horns on a slide in her hair and a two-foot long pronged tail sewn into the back of her skirt.

They had decided within two bites of a tuna mayonnaise sandwich that they would go with American George and his offer of the film contract and, in order to be able to afford to stay in the city until filming started, they had agreed to work some shifts in the man's nightclub. He'd called the Bottomless Pit a kind of themed fun club with an SM floorshow but they hadn't reckoned on it being done out like a fibreglass cave with flickering red lights set into the walls and flames projected all over the ceilings. And they certainly hadn't reckoned on having to wear ridiculous devil costumes to be able to work there.

Now Jane and Marie were getting ready for the first shift having been told to report for work immediately. The club's head of security, an oily malevolent looking individual as wide as he was tall, big hands swinging at his sides like hatchets ready to fall, was pacing up and down as he explained what they were expected to do and what they, by no account, should not do. Yeah, talk to the customers alright. Smile. Be their friend. Don't let 'em touch you. No way. We got girls for them to touch. Professionals. They

<151>

handle it. You two… you two just look as pretty as you can. Then he pointed them in the direction of the the little metal door at the back of the bar that led down to the dressing room and told them what their jobs were for tonight at least. Marie was to work the door, sat in a coffin size hole in the wall with a little window to look out through, and to tear each customer's ticket after they'd paid. Jane was to be behind the bar, fixing the drink orders that the girls who were working the tables brought to her.

Jane pulled Marie's tail. Hey I think this kind of suits you.

Well I think we look ridiculous. Shit. Do people really like this kind of pantomime? Men are such dumb animals. I mean they truly are pathetic.

A couple more girls came in and stripped off their jeans, teeshirts and sweaters, and began transforming themselves into part of what American George had termed his troupe of Devillettes. They sat on a pair of vinyl top stools and shared the same small bulb-ringed mirror that hung on the wall above a chipped white formica dressing table, fixing their hair, their eyes, brushing on lipgloss. While they got ready they introduced themselves to Jane and Marie as Carla Carnella, a dark skinned American Italian who spoke with a thick chew-gum New York accent and Leslie Kartovel, whose face and arms were covered with freckles and who wore her red hair in pig tails and had been born in Germany but had lived in Holland since she was five years of age.

Marie asked how they had come to be working in the club, and how was it? I mean, no disrespect to either of you but it seems like there are better places you could get a job. Jane said to ignore her friend and that it was just she didn't like any kind of uniform but Marie butted in saying that this wasn't any kind of uniform.

Leslie and Carla smiled and then looked at each other and then Carla fixed Marie and Jane with weary kohl eyes reflected back from the mirror where she was finishing up with her lipgloss. Her

<152>

mouth made a big O shape and then she kissed a paper napkin, screwed up the red stained tissue and dropped it to the floor. She turned on the stool to face them. Looked them up and down. Well darlings. I suppose I could ask you both the very same question.

Jane started telling her about American George and the film but she was interrupted by Leslie who was shrieking with laughter. When she finished laughing Leslie apologised and explained that she'd heard the same story a hundred times before.

Marie took a pack of Silk Cut out of the bag that she'd stashed in the corner of the room, lit one up, then offered the pack around. So you're telling us there is no movie? It's just some scam to get people to work in this place.

Carla took a drag on her Silk Cut, crossed her legs, got her tail caught between her knees, pulled it clear then straightened out the hem of her skirt that had ridden up proving that she wasn't wearing anything underneath. No, that's not it. Sometimes there is and sometimes there isn't. You normally get the movie spiel after you've started at the club. I mean I'd only been here a couple of days when they told me they had this movie thing going and did I want a part. How about you Leslie?

Leslie was brushing on more mascara. She looked over. Oh. I got it the first day. Had them both on at me about it. Turned them both down.

Jane looked a little worried. She sucked hard on the cigarette, blew out the smoke. American George said the film was shooting later in the month. Are you telling me he was shitting us?

No, not at all. Well not definitely. They do make films. It's just I guess that they use those lines on everybody. If they got you here specifically to make a movie then that's probably what you're going to end up doing. I guess they can use girls like you. Don't worry. Just ask them out right.

Marie ground her cigarette into the concrete floor of the dressing room with her red patent spike heel. She leaned against

<153>

the door frame. Looked at Jane like I-told-you-so then turned to Carla. You said 'they'. We only met the one called American George.

Yeah. His partner. Nicolaas. They work together. Run this place. Then they have a couple of bars, a cinema, brothels, sex shops, and they have the film business. That's just the stuff we know about. They work a lot of things. Big things. They're good to work for. Pay well. They won't make you do anything you don't want to. Like Leslie said if you turn them down, that's it. They'll leave it at that. If you're straight with them, then they're happy. One time two of the girls from the floorshow were sick on the same night. They asked me and Leslie to cover and we said no, that's not our thing. They said okay, got some other girls in to cover. Didn't sack us, didn't do anything. Never mentioned it again. Some places you work you have to blow the manager every night just to get paid. Nothing like that here. They never touch us. No hassles at all.

Jane took another cigarette from the packet on the dressing table. She'd eased up a little. Things weren't as bad as they'd seemed. At least there was still a chance for the movie. It didn't seem like it had all been a bunch of total bullshit. She asked Carla whether she thought it would be possible to speak to Nicolaas or American George later on and Carla said that she was sure one or other of them would be around at some point and that they should all maybe go up into the club right now to see if they were there and so Leslie and her could show them around and maybe they could see that it wasn't such a terrible place to work. Leslie led the way along a corridor stacked with aluminium barrels and crates of used beer bottles and mixers and up the iron steps that led to the back of the bar. Jane and Marie followed, watching Leslie's tail as it swung from side to side in front of them.

<154>

Riddle's Rule

Loose Joints had brought two books along with him on this trip. The first was a paperback copy of Joseph Roth's *Legend of The Holy Drinker* which he had found on a tube train underneath a crumpled copy of Girl About Town somewhere between Swiss Cottage and Baker Street travelling south on the Jubilee line. As the book was so thin he knew that he'd have the thing finished before he'd really got around to starting it, so he'd decided to keep it until he was travelling home on his own and that way he would have plenty of time to read it through in one go and plenty of time to think about it after he'd finished it. Besides, the second book, and the one he was now reading as he sat in his hotel room sipping from a glass of iced blue label vodka and 7-Up, was too fascinating to even think of putting down. *The Weekend Gambler's Handbook* by Major A. Riddle gave the whole scoop on how to win at every kind of casino game. Loose Joints glanced over at the little travel alarm clock propped up by the side of the bed and was surprised at how much time he'd actually spent reading the major's book in what seemed like a few minutes since coming in from his walk around the flower market near the hotel.

He'd never been much for reading until his second spell inside, when he'd been holed up with a disgraced doctor. The doctor had been arrested while trying to sell blank prescription pads to an undercover police officer in a white convertible 7 Series BMW at the top of a multi-storey car park in Brighton. A well educated man, the doctor was always getting new books brought in to him from his many visitors. When he'd done with them he would pass them on to Loose Joints. By the time he was released Loose Joints figured that he must've read getting close to 150 books, which was 148 more than he ever remembered reading before. Previously he had finished a novelization of Star Wars and a

<155>

biography of the one-time world middleweight champion Randolph Turpin who'd ended up dead and broke in a backwards midlands town after his moment of glory against the legendary Sugar Ray Robinson.

The thing that sold this book thing to him was how he'd noticed that if he had his head buried in a book then the time just flew by. Still, he hadn't planned on coming all the way over here just to read, so he promised to himself that after a few more pages he'd get ready to head out for a walk around town and maybe make it down to that club.

Loose Joints took a shower and thought about Riddle's Rule #6 that he'd just read in the chapter titled Why You Lose.

'Most people double up when losing and, therefore, lose twice as much. The odds are exactly even that a losing streak will continue: the odds are the same that a winning streak will continue. Why double up when losing? The time to double up is when winning. The best you can accomplish by doubling up on your losses is break even—or lose twice as much.'

He thought about calling up Ray again to pass on this advice because the more he thought about it the more he still didn't like the set-up with the vanishing fish. But he realised that if Ray and Lisa had any sense at all then they would have split from the first hotel already and if they hadn't, well it was too late anyway. He didn't like the direction it was going at all. The deal he'd set up was now only going to complicate things. It was hard to get a handle on whether Ray actually was holding a winning hand. Whether he really should be asking Rudi to show. Was Ray winning or was he losing? He couldn't say either way for sure but he knew that for Ray, even if he'd have heard of Riddle's Rule #6, it wouldn't make any difference because winning run or losing streak Ray would always be going for broke.

Loose Joints let the water run over his face, pushed his long

<156>

hair out of his eyes, stepped out of the shower and began to towel himself dry. Of course there was always the possibility that the fish was some elaborate prank. He remembered a story he'd been told at an after-hours drinking club in Soho. A story that he'd always thought was slightly unlikely.

This guy had been caught skimming a fair amount of money from the take at a weekly poker game in Whitechapel and his boss, the man that ran the game, told him that the only way he could square this was to run an errand for him. He told him to drive to a lock-up garage where he'd find a body and he was to take the body and dispose of it somewhere. So the guy goes to the garage in the middle of the night and finds this thing all wrapped up in tarpaulin, bound with rope, tape and electric cable and he hauls it into the boot of his car and starts driving around looking for somewhere to put it. He's driving around and around, can't think of a safe place, can't think of any place. After fifteen or twenty minutes he thinks he notices that there's this car following him so he takes a right, and then another right and then right again. He's back where he started and this car's still behind him. He's panicking now. Somebody must've seen him in the garage. Somebody must've called the police. Sweating. The car's getting closer to him. How is he going to get rid of the body in his boot? He drives on for another few miles. He's thinking prison. Prison. Prison. Prison. Pretty near shitting himself. He still can't lose the tail. So he thinks fuck it. I'll just pull over. Maybe I'm paranoid and they'll just drive by. Maybe they're lost. Even if they are police they may not want to open up the boot. They don't necessarily know anything. Maybe they're bored and they just want to harass some lone motorist. So the guy pulls into a bus-stop and the other car pulls up right behind him. He hears the doors open, people walking towards him. He's staring straight ahead trying to compose himself. He's gripping the steering wheel to keep his hands from trembling. A knock on the window. A

<157>

voice asking him to get out of the car. He turns and it's his boss looking straight back at him through the glass. Big grin on his face. He walks the guy to the boot of his car, gets him to open it up, then takes a knife out of his pocket and slashes down the length of the tarpaulin. Sand bags and pounds and pounds of potatoes come spilling out into the boot. And the guy's face is white as a sheet and the boss man is just laughing, laughing, laughing. With some people you never can tell thought Loose Joints. Some people's sense of humour develops in very crooked ways.

Loose Joints got dressed, tied back his hair and drained the last of his glass of vodka, all the ice having melted and the 7-Up gone flat. Have to see what happens. Heads or tails. Who knows? He hoped it was going to go whichever way Ray was calling. Has to be one thing or the other. One thing for certain. You have to be pretty unlucky for the coin to land on its edge. Before he went out he called home one more time, hoping to get a chance to speak to the kid before he went to bed.

Cathal had already fallen asleep and he talked to his wife for a while, assuring her that he wasn't involved in anything and that he'd be home in a couple of days, not to worry, not at all. Give Cathal a kiss for me. And you too. I'll see you soon. Yeah, I love you too. Of course. Always.

<158>

Duplicitous Dialogue

Ray was swinging down the street, hand in his pocket holding on to the jar. Dark now, people crowded onto the pavements, sat outside cafes and bars, laughing, talking. Ray just heard babble.

He was thinking about what he was going to say to Rudi. How he was going to play it. He kept looking around him, trying to make sure that nobody was following him. He'd stop every few yards, glance over his shoulder and find himself staring eyeball to eyeball with someone else on the street but they'd just push past him and move on. Rehearsing his lines. Playing out the scene.

Yeah, so Rudi what's this shit you're trying to pull? What's this shit you've been spinning me about a fucking fish? Where's the fish? There isn't any fish. You got me hauling some other fucking thing, didn't you? I know what it is man. And I know it's gotta be worth more than two grand. So either you up the offer or you don't see that fucking precious jar of yours again. And I'm serious man. Fucking serious. I can lose something like that over here. Move it on bigtime. So what're you gonna do? Hey you fucker? What are you gonna do?

No. Wrong. Play it cool. Compliant.

Okay man, yeah we can sort it out. Five grand? Well I was hoping for a little more. Yeah, well you know it's worth more. I know it. I don't need the hassle man. Yeah. Okay I'll give it you back for that. Of course. It was just that I was a little pissed that you tried to dupe me. We can work something out back in London. Well I'm proving that to you. Yeah, I've got a brain. I'm using it. Rudi I'm telling you, I'm sorry for all the trouble but you've got to see it from my point of view.

It was at some point during the time he'd spent staring through the metal bars in the hotel room that he'd thought of a way to cash in his golden egg. If he could somehow convince Rudi that

<159>

he was prepared to hand over the thing anyway and if he could somehow con Rudi into giving him a positive ID on what was in the jar then maybe he could swing a better deal. Maybe he could convince this other crew to take it on for more than Rudi was prepared to offer. Looking out the hotel window, stars twinkling like some mad dot-to-dot and he was filling in the lines, trying to make the big picture.

Moving quickly, Ray followed the road along a broad canal and crossed at the third bridge he came to. Lights from cruising boats reflected long across black, flat water. A statue in the street with pigeons huddled around its feet. Some horrible Dixieland jazz blew from a corner bar. Ray looks in and sees bow-ties, straw boaters and striped waistcoats, lilting clarinet and the sound of glass dropped on a stone floor. And on. Into a side street that opens out wide and quiet. Ray looking for a street sign. Looking up at rooftop towers like some fairy tale scratching into the sky. Finds the street sign, checks the address. One road away from the Scorpion bar. Backtracks two hundred yards to the callbox he just went by. Taps the jar in his side pocket, hunts around for the phonecard in his hip pocket that he'd bought from the hotel desk clerk. Lights a cigarette. Calm. Takes a drag. Calm.

Okay Rudi it's me. Don't say anything yet. Now we have an interesting development here don't we? It would seem to me that you've been playing me as some kind of fucking idiot. Dicking me around. Are you going to tell me what's happening here? Are you going to tell me what the real fucking deal is?

Rudi sat behind his desk, on top of which were stacked piles of notes, six inch towers of fifties and twenties. Across the desk from him two men in linen suits, looking like brothers, each with an open briefcase on their lap. Rudi held his hand over the mouthpiece and told them to go wait outside, or go downstairs and get a drink at the bar. They put their cases on the floor and walked out the door. Rudi waited for the door to close, took a sip

<160>

from his coke float then uncovered the mouthpiece. Smiles. Hmmm. Ray. I was wondering what had happened to you. I was informed that you didn't make the appointment and, of course, I have to say I was a little worried. But, now you've called I'm sure...

Ray moved further inside the callbox. Hunched up talking into the corner, catching the smell of a stubbed out cigar jammed down a crack in the side of the booth. Then mustering some menace into his voice, Don't start shitting me Rudi. Just tell me.

Rudi reached for the cigarette box, lit one, leaned back in his chair. Playing it simple. Casual. Friendly. Okay, Ray, okay. I think we can sort this out. I'll admit I haven't been exactly honest with you. But there was a reason for this, I can assure you.

Through the glass Ray watched a group coming towards him, drunk, arm in arm, singing loud. He asked what the reason was then missed the first part of Rudi's reply as the group passed the booth still singing.

You see Ray. I didn't want to worry you. What I was asking you to do carried a certain amount of risk.

Yeah, more than two grands worth.

I can't deny it. Can't deny that at all. But remember, you do owe me. That's how it started.

Right okay look Rudi. I don't want the hassle. I'll play it straight with you. You don't bullshit me and I won't fuck you around anymore. You tell me the deal with the jar, how much you're going to up my fee by and we can come to some arrangement.

Now you're talking Ray. You could go far with me. I'm always looking for people who show initiative.

Ray squatted down in the booth, leaning on his heels. Rocking gently. Rudi. I said no bullshit. First I want to know what's in the jar?

Rudi smiled at the end of the line and fingered the coil on the

<161>

telephone. Tell him. Why not? It won't matter for long. A ten minute conversation and it all pans out. Rudi playing it like Brando in some movie, hands waving around his empty office. Ray's hand cupped around a cigarette, De Niro feigning boredom. A stifled yawn. Both acting it out. Delivering lines. Never missing a cue.

Right Ray. This is it. This is how the whole thing runs. I am involved with a number of personalities in Europe and in Amsterdam in particular. We have very close business ties. Very close. And of course I'm very happy with the products that they supply me. Obviously though, and you'll appreciate this, it is in my own interests to stay ahead of the game. We're always looking to product improvement. So in this particular instance I've been involved with some R & D...

Ray wondered if this was supposed to be for real. Then figured that it must be and saw pounds, dollars, guilder spinning in front of his eyes. Wait until he told Lisa about this. Wait until Loose Joints heard...

Research and development in the UK by an American for intensive manufacture in mainland Europe. Rudi throwing money at this chemist and he comes up with a magic cluster of ...benzene rings, methoxys, 2-carbons, 3-carbons, amino group chains... On and on. Rudi figuring that it didn't matter saying this. Ray would be out of the picture sooner or later. He'd sweet talk him into giving up the jar, lure him with the promise of money and then...

Okay Rudi, I think we can come to some arrangement... Ray needed details, pleading ignorance he said... Let's cut the shit. I deliver if you tell me it all.

Rudi played it straight, so straight Ray thought he had to be lying but what the fuck he'd go with it...

Simply stated it's a new drug, a new psychedelic drug which, and this is of particular interest to me, makes it a perfect club drug, makes it a highly desirable drug and a very expensive drug.

<162>

What you're holding is the first sample. The very first untested prototype solution...

Ray clenched his fist. Unbelievable.

You see Ray, before we can move into mass production over there, a sample needs to be delivered to my associates who'll run some tests, try it out on a few people. Giving them a sample makes the whole project run so much more smoothly... And the formula would take upwards of a week to manufacture. Be like handing it to them on a plate. The sample is some kind of safeguard. Some insurance.

Ray paused. Waited. Money?

Now I appreciate that I haven't been completely honest with you, but I think we can sort this out. If you go ahead and deliver the jar as previously arranged I will ensure that there's a four grand fee waiting for you. I'm doubling up Ray. A show of goodwill...

Feint, parry, block. Ray shuffling. I'm thinking about it. It sounds possible. I don't see why not. It's got to be worth more than four grand though. Tell me. How much is the jar actually worth?

Ray, it's priceless. Figure you're holding the equivalent of 10,000 hits at around twenty to thirty notes a hit, final figure is upwards of two hundred grand. But of course it'd be worth much more to the right people. I'm telling you it's revolutionary. Truly remarkable...

Ray blew a silent whistle. Alright, for ten grand I'll have it to your man within the hour.

Rudi smiled. Hooked and landed. Ray I like you. You've got a deal. Be glad to have you on the team. You've still got the address? He's still waiting.

We can do it then. Call him. Tell him to get the money ready. I'm on my way. Last thing though. What was the shit about the fish fight? What about the video? Ray remembered the glass bowl

<163>

and the men in dinner suits.

Rudi laughed. Of course. The fish. Well that is something that I do. An idle diversion. Something different to pass the time. Next main event is in the Holiday Inn at Brent Cross. You'll have to come along. Be my guest. Really, Ray, it's a remarkable thing. And of course I knew I wouldn't have been able to get you to carry something over for such a small sum if you'd have known what it was. You didn't worry about a fish. You need never have known.

At the end of the phone call Ray touched the jar. Like the grail. Like everything he and Lisa had ever wanted. Like never having to go home again. Like never looking back. Opportunity. A golden egg. He tried calling Loose Joints at his hotel but his line just rang and rang. He backed out of the booth and walked towards De Schorpoien.

At the end of phone call Rudi buzzed the intercom to call Frank. Rudi told him it was sorted. Get them ready at the American Hotel. We'll be getting the stuff back and then they can slice him up. I'm going downstairs to find those two guys. He gestured to the money on the desk. Put this in the safe. If Harry calls then tell him we know where Ray is. And tell him to go to the American too. And that Rootboy. They can do them all at the same time. Jesus. Wish I could see it happen. Sweet goodbyes. The fuckers have wasted so much of my time.

<164>

A Lullaby Of Noise

Lisa lay on one of the beds in the darkened hotel room. Drifting in and out of sleep. A lullaby of noise from the street below. She stared at the wall following a crack from the skirting board up to the ceiling like a black marker had inked a line over the grey. Thinking about Ray. Eyes closed. A house, Ray and Lisa sitting at the kitchen table peeling oranges. Sunshine. Blue sky. Skin warm in teeshirts and shorts. Ray's arm stretching over the wooden table towards her. Touching hands. A cat sleeps in the open doorway. Basking. Birds on the fence. Singing.

A knock on the door. Lisa opened her eyes. Jumped up. Switched on the table lamp on the floor by the side of the bed. Looked at her watch. She walked towards the door, reached down to unlock the deadbolt. Okay, Ray I'm coming. She started to unfasten the door chain. Just one second. The door pushed towards her, hit her shoulder. Straining against the chain. Lisa gasped. A hand shot through the opening, reaching around for her, fingers grasping air then grabbing the chain and pulling at it. Lisa pushed all her weight against the door slamming it hard against the man's forearm. He cried out. Tried to free his arm. Pushed the door back open. An inch and he wrenched it free. Silence for a second, then he charged at the door. The frame splintered and the four screws holding the chain leapt out. Lisa jumped back and the man came tumbling through and fell into a heap on the floor. He got up, looked around the room, saw Lisa and started moving towards her. A fixed and crazy grin, scar running down the side of his face.

Okay bitch. Where's your boyfriend?

Lisa backed away until she was standing under the window. Rootboy closed the door behind him. Stood there. Started moving towards her again. Lisa looking around for a weapon, hands

<165>

feeling across the table top. Eyes fixed on Rootboy. He's not here. What do you want?

I want your boyfriend and I want the jar.

Lisa's fingertip touched the dried petals of the flower drooping from the empty Perrier bottle then pulled away from it like it had burned. Not yet.

Rootboy was just standing there. Waiting. Now he was sure that they were on their own he knew he could take his time. Have some fun. Sure thing they almost fucked up earlier but they were close to doing it right for Rudi now. Close to Ray. If he held on to the girl then Ray would surely come to him. The freak with the nose-ring at the station had told the truth. Forced desperate luck that they'd found him and that he'd remembered talking to Ray and Lisa. And the desk clerk remembered and it didn't take much arm-twisting for him to spill what room they were in and that the man had just gone out but the girl was still in as far as he could say. Oh I'm sure she'd like a surprise visit from an English friend. Yes, go right on up. No. When he comes back I won't tell him you're here. I wouldn't want to spoil your surprise. Rudi would be happy now. Harry and Rootboy had turned it around. Didn't even need to go calling on Rudi's cavalry.

Here he was surprising Lisa while Harry waited in the street so he could follow Ray up to the room when he came back. Rootboy told Lisa not to make a move or he was going to have to tie her up while they waited for Ray to come back. Man, he's been causing us so much trouble. Serious. Thinks he's a real hot shot with his beautiful girl and everything. He's the kind of guy that pisses me off. Big time. Thinks he can run around doing whatever he fucking well wants and no one can touch him. He's the type of guy that thinks his shit tastes like wedding cake.

Moving closer to Lisa. Backed up against the wall. Ten feet away. Moving around the bed. Five feet away. Two feet. She reached across and picked up the bottle. Not a good idea Lisa.

<166>

Close up. He reached for the bottle and she swung it hard. A blurred green arc to Rootboy's head. It glanced off his temple and he stepped back a little. He dived towards her but she was quick, stepped sideways, jumped over the first bed.   Rootboy   was slightly dazed but he put it down to the smoking earlier rather than the blow to the head. Play it rough, it could be even more fun. A good excuse to really hurt her. Lisa was thinking about making it to the door. Rootboy jumped over the bed at her, cracked his shin on the iron frame knocking him off balance. He fell towards her. Lisa swung the bottle again. This time it caught Rootboy across the forehead as he came forward. Hard. The bottle shattered in Lisa's hand and she almost dropped the jagged neck but held it tight. A shard of glass sliced into her palm. She moved closer to the door.

Rootboy roared that she was a fucking whore. A fucking dead whore now. Standing up. A cut on his head, blood trickling down his face, running along the scar like it was a gutter. He touched his forehead pulling his hand away red and wet. He dived at Lisa again. She held out the jagged bottle in front of her. She side-stepped again but held her hand out steady. Rootboy crashed into it. The glass hacked into his stomach and as he hit the floor the impact drove it further in.

He screamed, then lay still, face down. Lisa picked up the bedside table lamp, held it with both hands, then swung it down on the back of Rootboy's skull. She hit him again. Harder still. Felt his cranium give a little under the heavy metal base of the lamp. The cable pulled from the wall and the room was in darkness. She felt blood spurt up her arm and soak into the front of her shirt. She waited. Her eyes getting used to the light leaking in through the window. She watched the blood dribbling from the wound. A dark stain spreading across the carpet from under the body. A terrible stench of blood and piss and shit.

Still.

<167>

Lisa switched on the light at the wall and moved over to the corpse. She grabbed the body by the shoulders and turned it over, tearing Rootboy's jacket as she moved him. A button popped off and wheeled across the floor, hit the skirting and stopped. The eyes stared straight ahead. The mouth fixed in a crooked smile. The neck of the broken bottle was buried deep in Rootboy's stomach. The dried, mangled flower, stem crushed, still drooping from it.

Lisa felt like vomiting. She felt like crying. And she was shaking. Talking to herself. Oh Jesus Christ. Oh Jesus. Oh Jesus. She had to get out of there. Somebody must've heard the noise. She looked at the body on the floor and remembered Ray telling her about a man with a scar and about how he was always with somebody else. Now this other person had to be nearby.

Lisa grabbed her bag, picked up her coat and buttoned it up. She was drenched in blood. The coat covered the worst of it but her palm was gashed from the broken glass and dripped red over everything she touched. She took a scarf from the bag and wrapped it tightly around her hand. She ran out of the door and started down the stairs.

When she reached the last flight of steps she stopped. From where she was standing she could see a group of people clustered around the desk clerk complaining about the shouting and banging that they'd heard from an upstairs room. Telling the guy he should call the police. It's like somebody was getting murdered or something. Well if you're not going to call them then I will. A bearded man reached across the desk to the phone. The desk clerk wrestled it from him. I don't think we need to get the police involved. The bearded man said that he was going to go outside and find a policeman anyway and that somebody should go up to the room right now and see what the fuck was going on.

Lisa crept down the remaining stairs one at a time, keeping an eye on the argument around the desk. She reached the bottom

<168>

step and then ducked through a door marked PRIVATE. She moved through a cramped, jumbled office space then through another door, down a short dark corridor until she found herself in a concrete yard full of dustbins overflowing with paper and waste food. She opened a wooden gate and found herself in an unlit alley behind the hotel. She ran away from the hotel and into the first bar she came to. Went directly to the toilets and washed up, changing out of her blood soaked clothes then wedging them into a little cupboard of bleach and brushes underneath the sink. She sat down on the toilet seat. Her whole body felt like lead. Ray where are you, you bastard? Where are you?

When Harry had seen a bearded man rush past him into the middle of the street shouting, Police! Police! and trying to flag down a passing car, he'd run into the hotel and up the stairs.

Now he had tears in his eyes as he leaned over the bloody body of his friend. Don't worry man. I'll kill the fuckers. I'll kill them for you. There was nothing he could do other than pull one of the grey blankets from the bed to cover Rootboy's body.

Harry got up to leave, then noticed a crumpled street map lying on the floor. He picked it up and saw the red pen mark on it and a time written along the margin. He wadded up the map and stuck it into his pocket. When he turned to go out the door, he was blocked by the desk clerk and two other men. He spread his arms out in front of him, palms upwards. It wasn't me, man. Don't think it was me. I had nothing to do with it. As the men rushed him, he ducked and ran headlong towards the door. Crashing past them and on. Running down the stairs, taking three at a time. Out into the street and sirens coming closer.

<169>

A Night In The Hole

Taped music. Synthesised easy listening, computer strings, metronomic beat. And loud. Washing through every corner of the cine-flame licked club. Filling every crevice of fibreglass rock. Lights dimmed and a spotlight cut through a fog of cigarette and cigar smoke onto a heavy red curtain that covered most of the end wall. The curtain opened onto a round stage, spotlight dead centre. Two girls in devil costumes moved into the light. The first girl held a three pronged fork, the tip of each prong in flames. The second girl pretended to lick the flames then rubbed her hands over her body, sliding them over her breasts, between her legs, writhing to the floor in mock ecstasy. The girl with the fire undulated over her, waving the fork. Flames flickering. The girl on the floor loosened her dress, freed her arms, threw the dress across the stage. Now she writhed naked, pushing her body upwards, her hips grinding towards the flames. The music grew louder. Electronic brass coming in. A projection of lava flow lit up the back of the stage. Bubbling red rock hissing silently. Slowly. They were both naked now. The flaming fork propped up on the stage as they moved underneath it. Sucking on nipples. Legs spread and licking tongues.

Jane felt a tap on her shoulder. Carla held a tray in her hand. Clinking empty glasses. She pulled out a pad of paper, tore off the top sheet and passed it over to Jane and told her to get a move on. You don't have time to watch the show. Come on. Get this order.

Jane took the paper and reached down to the glass-fronted fridge by her feet. She took out three bottles of beer then she took a couple of shot glasses and filled them, placing them on a tray with the bottles, then poured two straight large White Horse whiskys from the bottle behind the bar. She put the tray down in front of Carla. I think they're good don't you? I mean

<170>

it. They're working well.

A roar from the tables near the front as a third girl walked onto the stage naked except for a fat, glistening, red vinyl strap-on.

Carla picked up the tray, Seen it before darling. Seen it all before. She turned and carried the tray back out between the tables that were staggered around the club, each standing on a wide circular mirror. She wiggled her backside so her tail swung briskly from side to side, arrived at a table and started passing around the order. While the floorshow was on they hardly noticed her, between acts the men would be just staring down at the mirrors.

Absolutely Sweet Marie was sitting in a tiny little cubicle smoking a Silk Cut cigarette and making her six inch Bob Dylan dance on the narrow shelf in front of her. Once every ten minutes or so a face would appear in the window and pass through his ticket for her to tear in half. She would pass one half back through and thread the other onto a long string that hung from a nail in the wall. She could hardly see the point in being there at all. She didn't take any money. Entrance was bought from the men on the front door. She just tore tickets. Between customers there was nothing to do but doodle on the edge of the single sheet of paper that contained the list of guests that didn't need to give her a ticket or stare out of her little window at the blank, red painted wall across the corridor. She wished she'd brought a magazine or something.

Twenty minutes passed without any action at all. She'd just run her midget Dylan through an up tempo version of *Jokerman*, beaten herself at noughts and crosses in the last square of space on the paper and was deciding whether she should smoke another cigarette now or if that would mean she wouldn't have enough left to get through the shift. She lit one up anyway. A face appeared in the window. Grey-haired but young. Marie figured on forty, forty-five. He was smiling.

<171>

Good evening. Marie isn't it? The man reached a gloved right hand towards her. As she shook it she noticed how cold it was, how the fingers didn't flex as she gripped his palm. I'm Nicolaas. You've met my partner already. Marie said she had and that she was glad to meet him and that a couple of things had come up that she wanted to discuss like what's the story on the movie? Is it happening? And Nicolaas nodded while she fired questions at him and said as a matter of fact he had some good news for Marie and her friend. Very good news I think you'll agree. We have secured finance somewhat earlier than planned and we'll be ready to start shooting in a couple of days. Come down to the office tomorrow evening and we'll give you the details.

Marie said that was excellent news and of course it meant she wouldn't have to work another night in this hole. No, I'm sorry. I didn't mean the club was a hole. Don't get me wrong. I mean this hole. Literally. And she waved a painted nail around the cubicle.

Nicolaas apologised and thanked her for putting in the time and said sure, she wouldn't have to work the next night. Neither would Jane. I mean you're stars aren't you? The both of you. Nicolaas said he had to go inside because he was expecting guests and had to play the host but it had been more than a pleasure to meet her and he'd look forward to seeing more of her. Marie leaned out of her window and watched him walk away, his leather gloved hand buried in his jacket pocket. He opened a heavy door at the end of the corridor. Noise and a flash of red light spilled through from the inner room until the door eased itself shut behind him. Marie sat back down on her stool and stared at the wall.

<172>

De Schorpioen

A blue painted sign in the front window. Ray looked inside. De Schorpioen was long and thin. Wood panels and brown leather booths ran the length of one side, stretching to the end wall in which were set two wooden doors with a Heineken mirror clock hanging between them. Along the other wall ran the bar. A dark wood counter, three big brass and ceramic taps, beer cloths and drip trays, a heavy green glass ashtray every couple of feet. Behind it rows of bottles, a tower of Coca-Cola cans, a neon sign for Budweiser, a poster for San Miguel, a large rectangular mirror with intertwined red scorpions painted around its wooden frame. Metal stemmed stools fixed to the wooden floor. There was nobody sitting on any of them. Ray looked around. The place seemed almost dead. Empty. All except for the barman who was leaning across the counter talking to somebody in a booth that Ray couldn't see into from where he was standing in the doorway.

He walked into the bar and sat on the first stool. Called over for a bottle of San Miguel. The barman reached down and opened a bottle without breaking his conversation then poured it into a stemmed glass, fixed a napkin around the base and slowly walked it over towards Ray.

The barman stood looking at Ray. Wiped his hand across the top of his shaved head, pushed his glasses up his nose. Ray slid the money across the polished wood. The barman nodded, scooped the money into his hand then leaned over the counter, speaking quietly. English with a strong accent.

Ray Gardner?

Ray nodded and took a sip from the beer.

Somebody is waiting to see you. Why don't you go on upstairs? You're expected.

Ray climbed off the stool and pointed towards the doors at the

<173>

end of the bar. This way? Which one? He left his drink on the counter and walked the length of the room. When he reached the door he turned and looked at the person that the barman had been talking too. The man sat in the corner booth, wearing a white suit, smoking a cigar and reading the front page of a copy of the International Herald Tribune. He kept on reading. Didn't look up. Ray checked his reflection in the Heineken mirror then went through the left door and climbed a short flight of wooden stairs towards another closed door.

Ray tried the handle and then knocked on the door. The door opened and a blond-haired man with a moustache asked him inside.

The room had the same wood panelling as the bar but was empty apart from a table and two chairs crowded into one corner next to a thick curtained window. On top of the table was a pile of papers and a mobile phone. The man shook his hand and introduced himself as George. Most people call me American George, you can call me that or just George, whatever you feel like. He laughed. Good to meet you. How you doing? How was Loose Joints? You're from London right? Great city. Marvellous. I love it there. Don't get there nearly enough. Every time any business comes up in London my partner's out of here. Straight onto the next flight. Always leaves me holding the baby over here. American George laughed. Ray smiled and looked at him. A vein pulsed near his left temple and Ray could see traces of white powder caught in the hairs of his nostrils and dusted over his moustache. American George wiped his moustache and sniffed as if he'd known what Ray had been seeing and then continued talking. I'm from Baltimore originally. Baltimore, Maryland. Course you probably could tell I was a US citizen from my accent. Then my name spells it out even clearer huh? Ever been to Baltimore? Ray said he hadn't. Baltimore has the best crab meat in the whole of the USA. Ever been to the USA, Ray?

<174>

Ray said he hadn't but he was thinking about going very soon.

American George went over and sat at the table. You'll love America. You really will. He offered Ray a seat, pushed out a chair for him and apologised for the surroundings. My partner and I have an office in town but we try to meet new people away from there. Just in case, you understand. This is just another space we use. No chance of us being disturbed. I bet you figured it was going to be some buzzing joint with a name like the Scorpion huh? He didn't wait for Ray to reply. Used to be, but we quietened it down. Suits us better this way.

American George asked Ray if he wanted a drink brought up from downstairs. Ray said he wasn't bothered, he'd get something later. But is it okay if I smoke? Ray had his pack out and was lighting up as he said it. American George gestured go ahead.

Okay. Loose Joints tells me you're interested in striking a business deal. Taking on some import duties for us. That right? Ray nodded. Did he tell you what it entails? Ray said that Loose Joints had explained it all pretty clearly but he let American George run the details past him. Asking if Ray wanted them to fix him up with a vehicle or did he have one here. And Ray saying he had one and passing the keys over the table and writing out the address where he'd parked it on a piece of paper.

Then American George laid it all out for him. The amount he was going to be carrying, the cut he could expect, how they'd have the car ready for him by the next day if he wanted to move quickly. Ray listened. Said it all sounded good to him and they shook on the deal.

Tomorrow then. That's okay with you? Call me in the morning and I'll tell you where to come to pick up the keys for the car.

Somebody knocked and George said to come in and the man in the white suit put his head around the door and told George there was a taxi waiting for him. American George looked at his watch and said he had to be going and why didn't Ray join him for a

<175>

drink later? He took a business card from his wallet and flipped it onto the table. Ray picked it up and looked it over. Gold ink embossed onto a red gloss card, picture of a demon in each corner.

That's a club I run with my partner. Come down later if you want. He stacked all the paper on the table and pocketed his phone, started towards the door. We'll get Joop downstairs to fix you up with a drink before you leave. On the house. Hope to see you later, definitely tomorrow. He popped a finger in Ray's direction and reached for the door handle.

Ray said he might just do that and slipped the card in his pocket. Then he asked George if he had time to discuss another deal. Something he might be interested in. George nodded and said Yeah, I should be going but tell me Ray, tell me, and he walked back into the room.

Ray laid it on thick. About this new experimental psychedelic. About the quality. He didn't mention Rudi, didn't mention how he'd come to be holding it. Just that he knew what it was worth and that he'd settle for twenty-five grand.

American George stroked his moustache. Well Ray, that's an interesting proposition you're putting to me here. Of course we'd need to see it. Where is it now?

Ray instinctively reached down to his pocket and touched the jar, thought better of it and looked relieved when he saw that American George hadn't seen him do it. He said he didn't have it with him, but that it was safe. He was certain of its quality and he was so totally and completely certain that it was something that American George had never even seen before that he was prepared to accept just fifteen grand when he picked up the keys to the car and that by the time he arrived in London with the E then George could've tested it and tasted it and could pay Ray the rest when he settled up the import fee. George said he was sure the figure of fifteen total was more conducive to business and Ray

<176>

laughed and said we're talking at least two hundred here. At the least two hundred thousand pounds sterling and maybe a whole mountain more if you can synthesise it yourself. You don't want it, I'll take it somewhere else.

Ray, I like your style. I think we can do some business here. One thing though. And I've got to know. Where did you get this from?

Ray had the answer down. Already played it out on the way here, and so then he explained about the friend of his with the laboratory in his garage and how he'd come up with this thing and given Ray a sample to try and then the lab had been busted and how Ray had held on to the sample and never tried it and couldn't find anyone in London that knew enough about chemistry to check it out so he brought it with him because he figured that somebody who was in the business of exporting and, he presumed, manufacturing E might be interested in diversifying with something new and better. And it all rolled out, Ray spraying bullshit over the table, so smooth and so even that he was believing it himself.

American George was looking happy. Said it sounded like definite potential. Said he'd talk to his partner and that tomorrow they'd have an answer for Ray but from where he stood right now he thought it might well be worth them taking a chance on him. We'll meet you and it's my guess we'll be slapping fifteen on the table. Dollars be alright? Equivalent value? Ray nodded. Then American George asked him if he realised it wasn't going to be too wise to carry that sort of cash back with him in a car stuffed with drugs. And Ray said he had a couple of people he could rely on to do that for him. Everything was safe.

American George looked at his watch again and whistled. Look Ray, I'm glad you brought this to me. Real glad. But I've really got to go. Got a taxi cab waiting. Like I said, get yourself a drink downstairs. I insist.

<177>

Ray followed him out of the door and down into the bar. George nodded to the man in the white suit and then told the barman to get Ray whatever he wanted then left Ray sitting back on a barstool waiting for the barman to pour him a vodka-7.

American George waved as he went out of the bar, then walked around the corner and let himself back into the building through a side door. He entered a little room behind the bar and positioned himself so he got a tinted view of Ray through the back of the scorpion mirror, sitting there looking straight back at him. He took his phone from his pocket and made a call.

Nicolaas. It's George. All he could hear was cheesy music and shouts and groans and glasses clinking. Nicolaas spoke, then the signal drifted and cut back in with the background noise muted. Can you hear me? Nicolaas it's George.

Yeah, sorry. It's a little wild tonight. I'm out in the back now.

Cool. Well I'm telling you man, you won't believe it. It's the same fucking guy. The guy your pal Loose Joints put forward for the run, it's the same guy that's fucking over Rudi with the sample. Incredible. Rudi faxed this picture over and I'd remembered the description you'd given me and I looked at the picture and I'm thinking this could be the same guy. The description. The picture...

So where is he now?

He's here in the bar. We were just upstairs talking about the E. I clocked him straight away. You know Rudi said that he was still expecting this guy to go to the hotel. He said he'd persuaded him to go ahead with the delivery. I've had people waiting there all night. Rudi wanted him taken out once he'd handed it over but then he comes here and I'm thinking why don't we let him take our gear back over and then when he delivers, Rudi can be waiting and he can do whatever he wants to him.

Nicolaas listened to George and paced up and down the corridor by the dressing room, then sat down on one of the stacks

<178>

of beer crates. George, I'm not sure I'm following this. Do we have the jar then?

No. He said he didn't have it with him. He may have been lying. It doesn't matter. He's meeting us tomorrow to pick up the car. By the way, get someone onto that. I've got the keys. Get someone to come and pick them up. When he meets us he's going to hand over Rudi's jar and, get this, he's expecting us to front fifteen on it. Yeah, what a fucking chancer.

George watches Ray gesture to the barman for another vodka-7. The barman crosses in front of the mirror and comes back with the bottle.

Alright so we'll definitely get it tomorrow?

Yeah. I think so. I can't see him going back to the hotel now. I waited and waited here for him. I made out I was going to leave to see if I could push him into some action. I was halfway out the door before he said anything. And I can't see him backing out on the deal with us. He's painted himself into a corner.

Have you got somebody that can watch him?

Yeah, that's arranged. Rudi says the guy's in town with a girl and they switched hotels on him so he's not sure where they're staying. Rudi had a couple of his boys shadowing him but they fucked up — he's more pissed about them than about anything else. Remember Harry? Yeah? Him and some friend of his. I don't know where they are now but Rudi told them to come and see us. When they do we're to take them out.

And what about Loose Joints? I mean, he's a regular guy. I like him. But he's really fucked up with this Gardner from what you're saying, George.

I don't know. I'll leave it to you. He's a friend of Gardner's isn't he? Might be better to keep him out of the picture. At least until everything plays out. Do you know where he is?

I know where he will be. He's coming here. Leave it to me. Nicolaas moved aside to let a couple of the Devilettes pass him in

<179>

the corridor on their way to the changing room to get ready for the next show. He nodded to them, waved, then continued talking on the phone when they'd gone inside. So if we've got to give him fifteen to get the jar, how are we going to straighten that out with Rudi? There was nothing in the deal that said we paid on delivery. Certainly not that much.

Yeah. I know it. If we want him to drive we'll have to give him something. I think we can convince him he'll get the rest later. I don't know, let's just put a few thousand down. When he gets to England with the gear he's going to get taken out anyway, so no payment. Simple. It'll balance. We might even get most of the front money back.

American George saw that Ray was down to the last mouthful of his drink, and slipping his packet of cigarettes into his pocket. Okay, he's moving.

Ray downed his drink, thanked the barman, left a tip on the counter and walked outside. The man in the white suit folded his copy of the International Herald Tribune, stubbed out his cigar and followed him.

<180>

Cavemen

Absolutely Sweet Marie was right out of cigarettes and getting more and more miserable by the second. She hopped off the stool she'd been sitting on for the past couple of hours and walked the two steps to the door of the cubicle and tried the handle. It was locked. Fucking Christ almighty. It's like I've been buried alive. She looked up at the little window and tried to gauge if she'd be able to squeeze through it. When she realised that the chances were so slim it wouldn't even be worth trying, she sat back on the stool and leaned her head out and shouted down to the front door for somebody to come and talk to her or something. Oh God I'm dying in here. For Christ sake this is inhuman.

One of the doormen came running up the corridor, fists clenched, eyes darting. Wide body, bulldogged, shaven head. He saw Marie's head sticking out, saw there was nobody else around and slowed to a walk as he approached her.

What the fuck's the matter? I thought you was being killed or something. He spoke slowly. Looking at her like he thought she was a piece of shit.

Man, I am dying. I'm dying of boredom, I'm dying of claustrophobia and I'm dying of nicotine withdrawal. Have you got a cigarette?

The man fished a crumpled soft pack of Marlboro Lights from his suit pocket and passed them to her. Hissed something she didn't hear.

Marie asked if it was always like this. She'd taken dozens of tickets about twenty minutes earlier but nothing since. The man told her how there was always a rush before the next show but between shows it got quiet. We take it easy outside. See before a show starts we're luring people in. Playing it up. Then when the show's nearly finished, like now, we take a breather. Then, in

<181>

about ten minutes, we'll be up again. Reeling them in. Just wait and you'll see all the tickets flying through.

Marie lit one of the Marlboro and took a long drag. Well that's all fine for you but I still can't see why I'm stuck in here. And you know the door's locked too. That's a fucking outrage.

The doorman fidgeted with the ring on his index finger. Straightened the creases in his suit trousers. Talked back to Marie like he really couldn't be bothered. The door's locked for your protection and the reason you're up here ripping tickets is so that the boss knows how many people have come through and whether we're ripping him off. They pay us, they get a ticket, you tear the ticket. The money we give him at the end of the night matches exactly with the number of tickets sold from the book and with the number of half-tickets on your string. None of us can pocket the twenty-five guilders and let someone in without a ticket because then they'd have nothing to give you and you'd shout about it and it'd cause a scene and... Simple. The boss'll trust you girls with anything, but us... he thinks any man is out to fuck him over.

Marie lit another cigarette straight from the end of her previous smoke. She asked the doorman if it would be alright to hang on to the packet and he grunted at her and walked back outside. She muttered under her breath calling him a fucking steroid caveman.

A few people were leaving, they passed by the window and Marie watched them. Mostly men in groups, a couple of women with their husbands or boyfriends. Everybody seemed happy, walking out drunk, or laughing, or hugging each other. Speaking in English, Russian, Japanese. Marie figured that a show must've just finished and that if the doorman was right then people would be coming through the other way at any minute. She flexed her fingers, cracked her knuckles like she was about to do something important. Held her hands out in the air in front of her, paused,

<182>

frozen, imagining she was waiting for a buzzer to sound and she'd have to burst into action. She held the pose for a couple of seconds then slumped back onto the stool, leaned her elbows on the shelf and looked over at the wall. Eyes glazed.

Oh hello. I'm a guest of Nicolaas. I think you should have my name down on your list.

A man with red hair tied back in a ponytail was leaning into the booth pointing at the paper on the shelf. The doorman was hovering behind him. Marie held the list away from him and asked his name.

Tommy Rourke but it'll probably be down as Loose Joints. That's what everybody calls me.

Marie found the name and looked over to the doorman, nodding that it was okay. She put a tick against Loose Joints' name. You can go on through. Nicolaas is inside. I saw him earlier. Marie watched Loose Joints disappear down the corridor thinking how cute he looked.

Loose Joints blinked a couple of times in the dim red lighting and then picked his way through the tables to the bar. He shouted for a vodka and ice hoping to be heard above the music, then he leaned on the bar and scanned the room looking for Nicolaas.

Your drink sir. The bar girl tapped him on the shoulder and he dug out a ten guilder note and passed it to her, took the drink and turned around to carry on looking for his man. He couldn't see him sat at any of the tables nearby and he wasn't among the half dozen or so huddled around the bar. He turned back to the counter as the bar girl was sliding his change over on a small black plastic tray. With a gesture for her to take the change, he leaned over so she could hear him, and asked, You haven't see a guy called Nicolaas, have you? Do you know him? He owns this place. I'm supposed to meet him here.

<183>

The bar-girl said Sure, of course I know him, he's around somewhere and then called across the bar to a colleague. Hey Jane, have you seen Nicolaas? Some friend of his is here.

Queen Jane Approximately, who was relishing all the attention she'd been getting in her blood-red devil's outfit, sashayed over to Loose Joints and told him that she'd seen Nicolaas just a few minutes ago disappearing out back to take a phone call and that she was sure he'd be resurfacing in just a little while.

Loose Joints had downed the first drink and he shook the ice in his glass indicating that he was ready for another. Jane took it, poured out a measure and brought it back to him. There you go sir. If I see him I'll tell him you're waiting. Then she took the ten guilder note from Loose Joints' hand and rang it up and put the change straight into the tips jar sprouting notes with coin roots next to the till. She winked at Loose Joints and then walked down the bar as Carla approached with another tray of empty glasses.

Hey LJ good evening! Nicolaas clapped his hands and led Loose Joints from the bar to a free table with a 'reserved' sign standing on it. He called over to one of the girls to fetch some drinks and then offered Loose Joints a cigar from an engraved gold case. So you're here. It's good to see you.

Loose Joints puffed on the cigar and looked over at Nicolaas. His grey hair immaculately cut. Still wearing that single leather glove. Yeah, Nick. Didn't think I'd ever make it over here. It's been good though. This is some place you've got.

Nicolaas laughed. We do our best you know. Hey why don't I fix you up with a little company for later on? He dug Loose Joints in the rib with his gloved hand. Hard. Loose Joints winced. Nicolaas had taken off the glove one drunken night in Soho. Showed him his fake hand. What happened? Was it an accident? Yeah. Sort of. Course this is just temporary. I'll get one that moves later. For now I've just got this. And he waved the thing, heavy plastic, fixed fingers, unnatural fleshtone.

<184>

What about it? A little action. If you know what I'm saying and I think that you do.

Loose Joints shrugged and said he'd think about it but, to be honest, he was happy enough just looking. And his eyes looked down to the mirror on the floor as the girl arrived with the tray of drinks, bending over the table, short skirt flaring so the reflection in the floor mirror was clear as a centrefold. So did Ray get to you? Is it sorted?

Nicolaas waved the girl away and slid a drink over to Loose Joints. I think it's going ahead. I didn't see him personally but George, my partner did. They had a very fruitful meeting.

Loose Joints knew better than to try asking much more so he just started talking about London and asking if Nicolaas was coming over soon. Nicolaas said that maybe he was, he couldn't say for sure. You know how business is. Things come up and you have to drop everything and get going. Loose Joints asked him if his business in London was solely connected to the deliveries of gear and Nicolaas held his hands up. You know I couldn't say. Hell, you'll be asking me who I'm delivering it to next. You know better than that. Loose Joints apologised and said he didn't mean to be out of order it was just conversation. Just talk.

A couple more drinks arrived and the next show started. Loose Joints watched over Nicolaas's shoulder as the girls danced with flames then fucked each other with dildos doused in petrol like some kind of bizarre fire-eating. When it was over Nicolaas, who'd been silent through most of the floorshow except for saying a few hellos and shaking the hands of people who came over to the table, asked if Loose Joints felt like going on somewhere else. Maybe we could go for a meal or something? If you want we could go and visit a couple of real life angels that I know. Loose Joints said that sounded okay to him. He was hungry. Well we'll eat first, then see what happens.

Loose Joints watched the city roll by through tinted glass,

<185>

digging strange streets and green vein waterways as Nicolaas drove and pointed out various sights. The car pulled up on the bank of a wide canal. Floating in the darkness were a number of boats, lights through small windows bobbing gently. Nicolaas got out of the car and went around to open the passenger door. Loose Joints climbed out and stood on the street, leaned against a street lamp. Where are we Nick? I thought we were going to a restaurant.

We will be. I just have to make a visit. Follow me.

Nicolaas led Loose Joints down a narrow jetty until they were standing on the deck of one of the boats. He opened the cabin door with a key from his pocket and stepped into the blackness. Loose Joints followed him through and stumbled up against a table or something submerged in the dark. He was feeling uncomfortable. Unsure. He cursed himself for having drunk so much and letting his guard down. What the fuck were they doing on this boat? Shit Nick. What the fuck are we doing here? Aren't there any lights?

<186>

Midnight Cold

The smoke came pouring out of the doorway like the place was on fire. Caught in the neon light it glowed pink, then blue, then drifted away up into the night. Lisa eased her way through the crowded doorway and pushed through to the bar. All along the wall was a mural of a giant pig, little white feather wings on its back flying through a rainbow hoop and a sky of multicoloured clouds. Within a minute a young girl came up and asked if she'd like any hash and Lisa said no thanks but that she could do with a drink.

She sipped on the double J&B and felt its warmth flowing into her. She was still shivering. Her skin was cold, tingling, like she'd come inside after having been out walking in a snowstorm. She'd eventually managed to get up from the toilet and make it through into the first bar she'd run to, but when they got a look at her ash white face, the people there thought she'd been fixing in the toilet and had kicked her out into the street. She'd moved on quickly putting space between her and the hotel and Rootboy's body and the bloody clothing stuffed under the sink. Now she was feeling a little more composed. She still felt like she was ready to retch at any minute but she sank the whisky and slowly felt the shivers subside. This wasn't simple anymore. This was a whole new story. Deep shit. She and Ray were in deep shit and he didn't even know it. She'd tried calling Loose Joints but got no answer. She'd thought about waiting around outside the hotel to get to Ray when he came back but decided it was too much of a risk. The other man could be there. A hundred men could be there. Waiting for Ray, waiting for her. She even considered a taxi to the airport and a plane home but that would mean leaving Ray on his own. She had to warn him. She had to meet him at the museum in the morning. She was sure he'd show. He couldn't let her down. Not

<187>

now. Until then she'd have to stay out of sight. She looked around the bar at all the people. A sickly smell of burning bush and resin. She couldn't stay here all night. She finished up her drink, went back outside and looked around for a taxi. She still had 100 guilders in her pocket. She'd rent another room out of the city and wait until morning. As the taxi pulled away she willed a message to Ray to stay out of trouble until she saw him in the morning, to take good care. I need you baby. We're all we've got.

<188>

Harry Waits

And I'm gonna show those fuckers how it is. I'm gonna slice up the bitch and I'm gonna carve a new arsehole in Ray's throat for all of his shit to come out easier. And I'm gonna turn this around and Rudi's gonna say Harry, my main man, I knew you could do it, you had me worried for a while but I knew you were the man and I'm never wrong. And Rudi was gonna take him on permanent and everything would be sweet.

Harry had run straight out of the hotel and kept on running until he'd come to the museum marked out on the map. Now, in darkness, out of sight, huddled on a bench in the grounds of the neo-gothic building he waited, fingering a six inch lock-knife and taking dabs from a wrap of sulphate that he'd picked up earlier in the day from a hustler on Stationsplein. Had to keep awake. Had to keep alert. He was going to have to wait almost ten hours. Ten hours until the time jotted on the map. Maybe that was something else. He didn't know for sure if it meant they were going to come here but it was all he'd got. And he knew Rudi wouldn't want to hear from him until he'd got some action and finished the job. Calling up Nicolaas was a bad idea. He knew it. It'd be like handing over his head on a plate, 'fuck-up' stamped across the forehead. The only way out of it, the only way to make good was to find Ray and the girl on his own. Bring them in. If they were going to come here he thought maybe one or other of them would show up earlier but he knew nothing would happen until daylight at least. He only hoped he'd recognise the girl if she turned up on her own. He'd seen her with Ray a couple of times. Only once had he got a really good look. Fuck that was enough. He'd make her. He'd know her if he saw her again. And if they didn't show then he'd have to think of something else. He couldn't go back now. There'd be nothing good waiting for him.

<189>

As it stood everything looked bad. Rotten. Still, he couldn't think of anywhere else to go. He was ready to wait out in the cold. And the thrill of what he was going to do to Ray and Lisa when he finally caught up with them was enough to keep him going. They'd gone and fucked up his big test. They'd gone and wrecked it all. His friend's bloody corpse on the carpet. He'd pay them back.

<190>

The Runaround

Fifteen thousand pounds on the table. Another ten to come when he got to England with a car stuffed full of tablets worth a cool two hundred. Probably more. It wasn't as if he was going to count them was it? Could be any amount in there. So if it panned out right he was sitting on at least fifty-five grand. A fifty-five grand cut on maybe five hundred grand worth of business. And this was big business whichever way you looked at it. He'd give up the jar, bring back the gear and walk away with fifty-five grand. Ride off into the sunset with Lisa on his arm. Except would he be able to walk? He was on the verge of fucking over Rudi royally and he was expecting to be able to just slip away. If American George was as good as his word then the rest of his money would be waiting for him in a lay-by three miles outside of Dover. He could hand over the car, pick up the fee, turn right around and lead Lisa back onto a boat taking them to France, catch a train into Paris for a couple of days of making plans, then on to the airport and... Fifty-five grand. They could get pretty far on that. Then again... They could get even further gone with the whole lot. Shit. Pick up the car, pick up Lisa and drive in the other direction. Drive away with fifteen grand cash and a car full of E. Easy into Germany and off-load it wholesale. Minimum now one hundred grand. Doubling up for the same risk. Even now Rudi would want to kill him. Soon American George would want to kill him too. You can only get murdered once and each of them would have to catch up with him first. One hundred thousand pounds plus buys a lot of distance. And there's a whole world out there to get lost in.

Ray passed the statue of the little boy. In the distance a church bell rang out twelve chimes. He walked quickly wanting to get back to Lisa and tell her this new scheme. He walked towards a narrow alley that opened up between two shops, short-cutting

<191>

back onto a main street. Going past the shop windows he stopped to look in at the jewellery laid out on red velvet trays, lots of blank spaces where the expensive stuff must've been taken out and put in the safe for the night. This was all cheap rings, plated bracelets, paste and costume shit. He looked at the rows of necklaces hanging from a pole across the back of the window, trying to calculate the prices back into sterling. Real cheap shit. He moved away from the window then caught a flash of white reflected behind him. He turned quickly, saw the white disappear into a doorway. He waited. A few people were walking around, busier back in the direction that he'd come from.

Ray carried on down to the end of the dark alleyway moving towards the pool of light leaked from a lamp in the next street. At the end of the alley he turned a sharp right and ducked back into a doorway, squeezing himself up tight into the shadows until he could feel the jar in his pocket pressing up against the wall. Maybe he was being paranoid. He was thinking about the guy in the white suit sitting back in the booth at De Schorpioen. The flash of white in the shop window. Waiting. Looking back at the alleyway. Nobody coming. Maybe it was nothing. Then footsteps, a shadow stretched out from the mouth of the alley, back lit by the street lamp. The shadow stopped, then stretched out and moved across the pavement like a ghost followed by the man in the white suit who was looking up and down the street. Ray held still, pushing himself back further into the doorway. He could hear the man heavy breathing and then grunting. The man turned slowly until he was facing Ray. Staring straight at him. Can he see me? He must be able to see me. Shit. What's he want? Ray tried to press himself as flat as he could against the wall.

The man walked towards him. Never could shadow worth shit. Bluff it out. Mr Gardner. Sorry to startle you. I was just on my...

Ray moved out from the doorway. Stepped in front of the man. Kicked his boot out and caught him hard just below the knee cap.

<192>

The man shouted out and fell forward. Ray kicked him in the stomach on his way down and then he reached out to him grabbed him by the throat digging in his nails, squeezing, thumb pushed up against his larynx. Hissing, What the fuck are you doing following me? Don't your people trust me or something? The man spluttered and started talking in Dutch, face reddening, tears rolling down his cheeks. I told them what the deal was and we made arrangements. Now I know where I'm going to be. I know what I'm doing and I expect your boss to get everything into place for me.

Ray loosened his grip on the man's throat then let go so the man's head dropped back with a dull thud onto the pavement.

So fucker, you can go back and and tell George that I don't need any baby-sitting and that he'll hear from me in the morning as arranged. And you can tell him if he wants to piss around with tails or shit like that or if he wants to start giving me the runaround in any way then everything's off. Finished. I can go elsewhere. He knows it. You tell him and I'll call him tomorrow. Jesus fucking Christ, some people. And Ray stood up over the man on the floor, kicked him again with the point of his boot then moved on quickly down the street and up over a canal bridge, waiting halfway across it, looking back. The man got up, smoothed down his hair, coughed a little, spat on the ground and then disappeared up the alley back towards De Schorpioen.

<193>

The Hot Shot

Loose Joints heard a click. A torch beam danced around the room flashing up split second circles of a table, a chair, a small chest of drawers, green painted walls, bare floorboards.

What is this?

Loose Joints looked towards the light and then saw Nicolaas's plastic hand come crashing down on his face and he felt the floor rising up and it was dark again.

Nicolaas hauled Loose Joints up on to one of the chairs then opened up a drawer and pulled out a small zip-lock plastic bag. He laid out a syringe and a spoon, a piece of cotton wool. He rested the torch down on the table, sideways on so it shone across the objects, casting giant spoon and syringe shadows on the wall. From his pocket he took a prepared vial and broke it open into the spoon. He heated the spoon with his lighter, put the cotton in, none of this because he needed to but just to make it look right. He tied off Loose Joints' arm with a brown fake leather belt from the drawer then he drew up the heated liquid in the syringe and jabbed it into Loose Joints' forearm. Needle slid the vein. Plunged.

Loose Joints groaned. Nicolaas hit him over the head again with the torch and he fell out of the chair and slipped down onto the damp floorboards of the boat, needle still sticking out of his arm. Nicolaas shone the beam in his face. Loose Joints' eyes were open. Staring upwards. The eyelids flickered. Hot shot. Fade. Fade.

<194>

Red Light

Ray headed for the hotel. Back to Lisa. He turned the corner and walked straight into a crowd of people arced around the entrance to the place. Up ahead an ambulance, two police cars, lights flashing around and around, over and across the surrounding buildings. He pushed his way to the front and up against a police barrier. What's happening? What's going on? He looked up to the top of the building and saw bright lights coming out of the window of the room they'd rented. Guests peered out through the other windows. Heads out of windows right along the street. Hey what's happening?

A woman next to him told him there'd been a murder in the hotel. I live just down there. I heard shouting, then a police car pulled up. I couldn't really see from my window but then a few minutes later I heard more sirens and another police car and then an ambulance so I came out here to see better.

Ray looked back up at the window. Shit. What if it's Lisa. Fuck. Turning back to the woman he said, Do you know who it was? I mean who got killed?

Well like I said I was here right from the beginning and that man there… she pointed to a bearded man inside the cordoned off area, talking with a policeman who was taking notes… he told me it was an Englishman that got murdered. They're looking for a girl and the man she checked in with. They don't know if they did it but they want to talk to them. Somebody saw the girl running down the road behind the hotel. And there was another man too. A different one. He was in the room when they found the body but he ran away. They don't know who did it. But it happened in the girl's room and she's gone missing now. Look. Look. They're bringing out the body.

A pair of ambulance men carried the body out of the hotel on

<195>

a stretcher, zipped up in a body bag. The people gasped like they were watching some amazing firework display as the men lifted it into the back of the ambulance. Ray pushed his way out through the crowd and walked away down the street.

Jesus fuck. Rudi must've had people watching us all the time. The body must've been somebody on Rudi's side. But the woman had said there was someone else too. Lisa had been seen running away from the hotel. They didn't say anything about someone going after her so she must have got away. The thought relieved Ray and he knew that she'd try and make the meeting the next day. She didn't know if Ray would make it back to the hotel or if he'd find out what had happened. She wouldn't leave without warning him and she was wise enough not to try and find him out in the open. So she'd have to go to the museum. Somehow Ray knew that wherever she was she would be safe. She had to be.

He found another phone and called Loose Joints' hotel again but the receptionist told him that Mr Rourke had gone out some time earlier and he hadn't come back yet. Ray hung up and walked towards the centre of town. If Rudi's people were out looking for him then he'd have to stay sharp. Go where the most people are. Where it's busiest. The easiest place to lose yourself.

Walking along OZ Voorburgwal, coloured bulbs strung over the bridges like perpetual Christmas. Boats of gaping tourists drifting under them like a ride on a fairground's tunnel-of-love, floating down the velvet canal. Whores yawning behind glass reminding Ray of visits to the reptile house at the zoo. Languid as the lizards there.

A group of Asian businessmen in uniform pin-striped suits and patent leather shoes huddled around one of the windows. Pink fluorescent strip lights framed the dark-haired girl inside. She stared blankly out at the men and toyed with the straps of her bikini-top. Like children at the zoo, the businessmen tapped on the glass and laughed every time she moved.

<196>

Ray checked out the window displays in a couple of shops, multi-coloured condoms, tubes of lube and wonder sprays, all kinds of inflatables and black leather and rubber outfits. Shelves full of garish video boxes depicting females and males with faces covered in come and piss and shit. Disappearing fists, arms and feet. Chains and whips and nipple clamps. Animals on boxes, a horse cut from a children's farmyard picture book.

Street noise, shouting, raging neon and flash-bulbs. Ray walked past barkers imploring him to attend their real-fucking-live-shows, their razor-shows, their punishment-and-discipline shows. He walked up to a booth at the front of the International XXX Cinema and bought a ticket for twenty guilder, the man in the kiosk explaining how the ticket meant he could stay inside for as long as he liked. Ray climbed a narrow staircase, walked through into the small auditorium and took a seat on the empty back row tucking himself right into the corner. The place stank of sperm and disinfectant. The heads of half a dozen other people were silhouetted against the screen in front of him. Ray watched the reel play out until the two girls on screen were licking come off each other and the two men were standing watching them, hands on their hips, snide smiles on their moustached faces and half-hard dicks flapping in front of them. Darkness and then another reel started. Scratchy 16mm print, frame flickering, image shifting in and out of focus, white block capital titles, blurred lettering.

For a few minutes Ray watched a brown-haired girl trying to get a dog to mount her and then he closed his eyes. Dogfuck played on and Ray tried to sleep to a soundtrack of yelps and moans and easy-listening electric guitar.

<197>

No More Yes

I know he didn't deliver. I know that... Well it's a coincidence isn't it... Yeah, but it isn't lucky for him... No. No. I totally disagree. You can't trust him. Fuck that. One of your people can drive it... Yeah. I have Harry and a guy called Rootboy over there... No fucking way can they. If it hadn't been for them then we'd have had this under control a long time ago... No, they've got to go. Haven't they called you?... No I haven't heard shit from them... I don't want to see either of them again. Wait. They'll make contact I'm sure of it. Wait for them and then get rid of them... Nick, I know what you're saying and I can understand George's thinking but look at it from my point of view. That piece of shit has been dicking me around all over, not just over there but over here as well... And how do you think I got him to agree to the delivery in the first place?... Right. Too fucking right. I can't allow it... No fucking way. Listen you stupid cunt, if you fuck up now then you're going to get it in the neck... Yeah. I said you... Fuck that. I'm not joking here... Yeah well when I spoke to George I was still under the impression that Ray was going to show. He was thinking he was hot shit, calling me, getting me to up the price and so I went along with it... Well he wasn't going to get a fucking penny was he? Soon as he'd turned up and handed over, some of your people were going to take him out... Yeah, remember that... So now I'm hearing that not only has this guy come to you and tried to sell you my gear but you've said 'Yes, certainly Mr Gardner' and offered him fifteen grand to hand it over... Too fucking right. Wouldn't you be?... You had him there and you just let him go... Listen. It's not about the fucking jar anymore. Even if it was you could've easily persuaded him to take you to it... Right. It's beyond that... Well I don't know any Loose Joints so that doesn't mean shit to me. I don't care about

<198>

that. I just want to know when Gardner is going to come to you?... And you're sure he's going to be there?... Are you certain?... Well I'm coming over. I'll be there and he better fucking turn up, Nick. I'm telling you. You better make sure he comes. I don't fucking believe this. No way. I just don't fucking believe it.

<199>

After Hours

After finishing their shift Carla and Leslie invited Marie and Jane back to their apartment for a few drinks. Marie and Jane sat next to each other on the blue leather sofa drinking glasses of red wine from the bottle Leslie had taken from the club. Leslie sat cross-legged on a pastel striped cotton cord rug skinning up a joint on the book of Far Side cartoons balanced across her lap. Carla was hunched over the portable CD player shuffling through the pile trying to find a certain album that she felt like hearing. She found the disc and put it in the machine. Guitar, drums, slide guitar. Jagger grunts and the Rolling Stones are dancing with Mr D.

How long have you been here? Marie was happy to be out of that hole she'd been locked up in all night and was looking to start any kind of conversation. She addressed the question to nobody in particular but Leslie, who was just putting a match to the joint, answered her.

I've been in this apartment nearly two years. Carla moved in about six months ago. We met at the club. Before that I used to share the place with an Italian girl whose boyfriend was a junkie. He used to come around here with his friends and steal stuff and wreck the place. And then they'd have these raging, howling rows that'd go on all through the night.

Shit. That must've been awful.

Leslie took a long pull on the joint, held in the smoke and passed it on to Carla. Then she exhaled and turned back to Marie. Yeah, it was. I had to get a couple of people from the club to come down and throw them out. Nicolaas arranged it for me. These two guys came in one night and threw the girl's boyfriend and one of his friends down the stairs. The girl was alright. They didn't touch her. I never had any problems with her anyway but she wouldn't come back after that. That's when Carla moved in.

<200>

Jane picked up the wine bottle from the floor and refilled their glasses. Carla offered her the joint and she took it but passed it straight on to Marie.

So Jane, did you get to speak to Nick about this film?

Yeah. Marie sorted it out with him. We're starting the shoot in a day or so. We've got enough money to last until then so I doubt we're going to work at the club anymore.

But you enjoyed it. I could see you were thrilled having all those men coming on to you.

Marie coughed, spluttering smoke around the room. She passed the joint back to Leslie, waving it away. Yeah, but I wasn't. Have you ever worked that ticket box? It's living death. Jesus. Like peering out of your own coffin.

They wouldn't make you do it two nights in a row. You should still work tomorrow. You'd be inside. It's fun.

No way. Like Jane said the movie starts in a few days and we're just going to relax until then. Shit hostess work I can get in London. No offence.

Carla turned up the volume on the player for the piano intro to Coming Down Again saying, Oh this is such a beautiful song. Wow. It almost makes me cry every time I hear it. And Leslie started ribbing her about how anything makes her cry like when they'd watched International Velvet a couple of afternoons before. Then Leslie asked Jane and Marie if they knew anything about the film they'd been hired for.

We don't know anything really. They'll have some clichéd weird shit for people like us to do I guess. I don't really care. The money's good and they're promising that they'll turn Jane here into a star which is the only thing she's ever wanted to be and has been her main topic of conversation since I met her.

Jane smiled. A film star's smile. Imagining signing autographs, going to parties and openings, magazine features, pictorials. It's like Marie said, who cares what kind of film it's

<201>

going to be? And what else have we got?

Later, drunk and stoned, Jane and Marie kissed Carla goodnight at the door, Leslie having already fallen asleep on the rug, head nestled on an embroidered scatter cushion. They whispered thanks and promised to let her know how the filming went then walked out into the street, weaving their way along the pavement back to their hotel as the sun yawned into early light.

<202>

Three Past Eight Thirty AM

8:30 Harry stretched and walked around a little more. Shadow-boxing, flexing his hands, running on the spot. An hour before, a policeman had told him to move on from the bench and since then he'd been pacing around trying to shift the stiffness out of his body. People passed him by on their way to work, nobody paying much attention. They probably had him pegged as a derelict, all red-eyed, crumpled clothes and stubble. He walked over to the information board outside the museum, checked once more that the place didn't open until ten and then crossed the street again to the cafe to get himself some more coffee and use the toilet. Buzzing from the sulphate, morning colours blurred on passing trams and cars, like a TV set with the tuning just out. He got his coffee in a take-out polystyrene cup, stirred in the last of the wrap and ripped in three packs of raw cane sugar. He took the drink to another bench hidden from the main entrance to the museum by some bushes and he sat and waited. Sipping on the sweet black coffee, looking through a gap in the branches, watching the entrance. Come on you fuckers. Come to Harry.

8:40 Lisa was up and dressed and staring into the mirror in her room, bloodshot eyes, dark rings and blotchy skin. She hadn't slept more than half an hour all night and then she was woken by a dream that had Ray falling from the roof of a high building and her running down the stairs seeing him fall past each window she went by and as she ran, stumbled and slid down endless stairs he'd still be falling past each window and the stairs went on forever and ever and just as she reached the ground and Ray's body was hitting the tarmac face down and she was crying and she turned him over and it was the face of the man with the scar and the broken bottle stuck out of his stomach, the flower all red,

<203>

bright and blooming and sucking up the blood from his wound. She'd woken up with a start in a dark room and couldn't think where she was. After that she'd switched on the light and lay there looking at the window, waiting for morning.

8:50 Ray came out of the cinema after having slept most of the way through the endless cycle of films. Every two hours or so, all through the night, an attendant had come around the auditorium checking on people, asking people who were nodding off or smoking, or doing drugs to get the fuck out of there. The second time Ray had been woken up he'd apologised and said that he was just resting his eyes. You know how it is. It's been a long day and I really feel like I need to unwind watching a few movies and I'm getting this thing for the blonde girl in Hostess Party you know what I'm saying. I just have to see her again. You don't mind? I bought my ticket. He waved the pink stub at the attendant. Okay man. Thanks. And he'd worked out that the attendant only came around at the end of the cycle which was when Dogfuck was starting up so he'd managed to half-sleep through the rest of the films and wake up when that film's guitar motif came up on the big speaker under the screen. Sit upright. Wave at the attendant. Yeah man, I'm still here. That girl man. I can't drag myself away. See you later.

Now sitting outside a cafe smoking a cigarette after a continental breakfast of coffee, croissant and orange juice, Ray was thinking about going down to meet Lisa. As long as she was there everything was going to work out right. He'd called American George first thing and had made arrangements to meet up at an address on Gravenstraat. George had apologised for the man having followed him the previous night saying how he'd acted without instruction, how the man hadn't intended to hurt Ray but had just been making sure no-one else did, just looking out for him. And Ray had said that he didn't ask for an escort and

<204>

he didn't need one. Yes, Ray I'm sorry. A simple misunderstanding. Forgive us. Ray said that was okay and asked if everything else was sorted and George told him how he'd talked to his partner and they'd okayed the deal on the sample and that the car was prepared and the keys would be handed over with the money. Looking forward to seeing you again Ray. Twelve O'clock. 19 Gravenstraat, I'll be waiting for you outside.

Lisa wasn't sure how long it would take her to get to the museum so she asked the receptionist when she went to the desk to settle her bill. The girl told her which tram to take, where to catch it from and that it wasn't all that far away. Lisa went outside, crossed the street and waited for the tram. When it stopped she checked with the driver that it was going to the right place and then climbed on board and sat squashed into her seat as a party of children on their way to the Artis Zoo threw rolled up paper pellets at each other and shouted and sang. She asked someone to tell her where to get off and when she found herself back out on the pavement she looked at her watch and saw that she was twenty minutes early.

Lisa figured that she may as well just go and wait inside and she walked towards the museum. When she reached the door a man gestured from inside that the place wasn't open yet and so she sat on the step and watched tourists take photographs of each other and feed scraps of bread to the pigeons that were milling around on the concrete slabs.

Harry saw the girl approach the door from where he was sitting. He got up from the bench and walked towards her. Casually. Slowly. Getting close up. It's her. Man, I couldn't mistake her. He came to the edge of the step and called over to her.

Lisa? Hey Lisa. She looked up and straight at him. Sure it was

<205>

her. Definite. Lisa, you waiting for Ray?

Lisa looked over at the man. Trying to decide if she should run. Did she need to? She looked at her watch. Still fifteen minutes until Ray was due. Hang in there. He'll come.

Lisa. Ray sent me. Come with me. I'll take you to him.

Lisa got up and walked over. Stopping far enough away from the man that he wouldn't be able to reach out and grab her. Yeah? I don't believe you. Where is he?

He had some business on. He couldn't get here himself. Follow me. I'll take you to him. He's waiting.

Harry gestured for Lisa to follow him and he started back towards the bench. She felt easier now. He hadn't tried to jump her. It must be alright. He's asking me to follow him. He's walking away. She followed Harry down a small path between some high bushes out of sight of the road and the museum entrance. He'd stopped ahead of her, waiting for her to catch up. She looked back hoping to see Ray. This guy. I don't know. Maybe she should wait. He had a London accent so he could be a friend of Ray's. Then again so did the guy that busted in on her the previous night. Ask him for proof. Something. Anything. When she reached him she was just about to speak when Harry grabbed her arm and twisted it behind her back. She gasped. He had the lock-knife out and held it up to her throat.

Okay. Listen. Not a single sound. Not a word. Try any shit and I stick you with this. He jabbed the tip of the blade into her neck. Lisa stood still. We're going to go for a walk and we're going to take a drive. So no fucking shit. You understand?

Now Harry had Lisa. He had thought he would just kill her and go back and wait for Ray but all the time he'd been walking around that morning he hadn't found any place to dump a body where it wouldn't be found within a few minutes. The police would be swarming before her body had even started to cool. And he didn't have time to take her away and get back for Ray. There

<206>

were people all over this place, even holding her with the knife was risky. He should've left her on the step, waited for Ray to show and then just gone for him. A wired night on a bench was no way to prepare, he knew that now. Still he had something. Something to bring back to Rudi and his friends. He could make this work. He'd bring Lisa with him and call Nicolaas, get him to send someone to pick them up, tell him that he'd found Ray and the girl and he had the girl with him and that Ray was on his way. Easy now. Mission accomplished and Rudi would be thanking him for salvaging such a tough job. Snatched it back in the last act. Now he just had to convince Lisa to come with him without squealing and causing a scene.

Thinking quickly, back to a million bad cop shows, he told Lisa about how they had Ray held up somewhere and how if he didn't get back to them with her, that would only cause Ray more trouble. So why don't you make it easy on everybody and come along quietly? I'm going to phone through and they'll be along to pick us up. I'm sure we can sort everything out. We're reasonable people. Lisa shrugged like she hadn't any choice anyhow and let Harry put the knife away and lead her away from the museum holding her hand and twisting on her little finger if she walked more than a pace faster or slower than him.

Ray crossed the road, walked up the steps and reached the museum door just as it was being opened. He asked where the cafe was and whether he had to buy a ticket just to use it. The man told him that the restaurant was right inside and that, yes, he did have to pay. Ray handed over seven guilder, picked up a museum plan and followed the signs to the restaurant. He wasn't surprised that he was the first customer and he chose a seat in the corner by the window that gave him a view of the whole place and let him look back across the paved area leading to the main

<207>

entrance. He sat reading through the museum plan while he waited for Lisa to show up.

Harry and Lisa were standing by a green phone booth at the side of a canal. They stood in silence, both watching cars approach them and then drive past and away. A white Mercedes pulled up alongside the kerb and the driver gestured for Harry to put Lisa in the back first and then get in himself. Lisa sat between Harry and a man with a blond crew-cut and tortoiseshell shades, who wore a Nike top and jeans. There was a screen between the driver and the back seat like in a taxi cab but Lisa could see the silhouette of another man through the dark tinted glass. After the car had eased back into the traffic Harry started talking excitedly, asking if they had other people on the way to the museum. I mean it. He'll be there. None of the men would answer him. He turned to Lisa who was realising that he'd conned her and that these men didn't have Ray at all. You bastard. You fucking bastard. Ignoring Lisa, Harry carried on trying to talk to the men then, after meeting more silence he turned back to Lisa. They don't speak fucking English. Jesus. Stupid shits. They're gonna fuck it all up. The guy with the crew cut looked over at Harry and smiled.

After driving for ten minutes the car took a right, turning into a narrow service road that led to a yard behind some disused warehouses. The driver got out and opened the back door and told Lisa and Harry to get out. They stood in the concrete yard, high brick walls on each side. The blond-haired man had the boot of the Mercedes opened and he politely asked Lisa if she would mind climbing inside. Lisa said that yes she would mind and why didn't they all go and fuck themselves. And Harry shouted at her to do what they said. Yeah, do it. Move it you fucking bitch.

The blond man grabbed a handful of Lisa's hair and dragged her towards the boot. She told him to let go and she'd get in.

<208>

Okay, okay I'm in. I'm going. Lisa curled up in the boot, surprised that it wasn't as cramped as she'd thought. She looked up and saw the lid closing down, light cut into finer and finer slices until it slammed her into darkness. She lay still and listened as she heard the passenger side door open and somebody get out. She heard Harry saying hello and then saying, No, you can't be serious. Put the fucking thing away man. It's not funny. No way man. This isn't funny. And then she heard a shot, a couple of sentences in Dutch, footsteps. The car doors closed and the vehicle started to move again.

An hour and three cups of coffee gone and Ray was beginning to think that Lisa wasn't going to show. Maybe the thing the night before had been too much. What did he really expect? If he'd been her and shit like that started happening he'd have been out of there. Long gone by now. He'd thought that maybe she'd have stayed around for him but who was he fooling? Shit. She gets thrown into something that she's never been involved in before. He tells her it's simple. It'll all work out. And the thing starts spinning every which way and she ends up with people tailing her, bodies in her hotel room and even the police are looking for her. Who was he trying to fool? Like he was God's gift and she'd be risking her neck to get a message to him? No way. She was smarter than that. And hadn't he told her to get going if things looked bad? Go back with Loose Joints. Yeah that was it.

Ray walked out of the restaurant and up to a public phone in the entrance hall. He scooped a handful of change from his pocket and called Loose Joints' hotel again. The receptionist put him through to the room and after the phone had rung unanswered for a half minute she came back on the line. I'm sorry sir, Mr Rourke isn't answering. Ray asked her if she could check whether he'd been in since last night and she told him that she

<209>

couldn't do that seeing as how the girl on the nightshift had already gone home and there was nobody else there who'd have any idea at all. Ray thanked her and told her that he didn't have any message to leave. That was that then. Loose Joints had gone and Ray's guess was that Lisa had gone with him. That would be okay. He'd make the meeting, pick up the money and the car and send for her when he got to Germany or wherever it was he thought looked best to move the gear. She had enough sense to stay out of Rudi's way. Loose Joints could take care of her. That would work. That would be the way it would be. Rudi had no contact with Loose Joints. She'd be safe with him. Rudi didn't even know he existed.

<210>

When The Ocean Meets The Sky

Ray turned the corner past a big old church, walked a little faster, hand in his pocket, wrapped tightly around the jar. Followed the street to a black wooden door with a tiny number 19 on a handwritten sign stuck next to it. Ink run from past rain. He looked up at the building and saw that right up to the top all the windows were covered in wire mesh. Behind the mesh were numerous broken panes of glass with boards covering the holes. Windows like black eyes. He pushed the door, found that it was locked and then pressed the lit button on a metal-grilled entry phone. American George's voice crackled through the speaker.

Hello can I help you?

George. It's Ray.

Ray. Good timing. I like that. You brought the stuff? Good. We're upstairs. Come through, take the door across the room on your left as you come in.

The lock buzzed and Ray pushed at the door and it groaned and swung open and he went inside. A large room painted black. Shades covered the windows adding to the gloom. Pushed up along one wall were a pair of kingsize beds. On top of these were a few chairs, a small sofa, some rolled up rugs. Across the room was another pile of stuff that was covered by a sheet. Then, in the far corner, a row of big silver lamps and a couple of yellow plastic crates with cables writhing out from them onto the floor. Ray crossed the room to the door that stood between a packing crate stuffed with clothes and fur coats and a cardboard box filled with porn mags and books.

Ray took this place as being some kind of studio. Probably another of George's enterprises. Maybe they used it as a front for the drug business. It seemed odd to him that George was inviting him in somewhere else. Say he got pulled by customs. How did

<211>

they know he wasn't going to go tell all about it? Dumb move. If he did get pulled, and one thing was for sure if it happened it wasn't going to be by British customs, but if he did then he could use all this to bargain his way out of some of the trouble. Maybe squash a fifteen plus sentence below five.

Fuck it. He was thinking about getting caught before he'd even started. No way Ray, that's not how it's done. Never did that before. Never. He was riding into paradise. Just think of that. Lisa and him. Money enough. Sweet. Wouldn't hurt getting all the information he could though.

He opened the door and climbed a flight of stairs to a long corridor that had film posters tacked up on the walls between a series of closed doors. The door at the end was open and he could see American George standing there waving him on. Hey, Ray good to see you come on in. Ray glanced at the posters as he walked down the hall. Mostly soft focus shots of naked women that Ray didn't recognise. Titles that Ray had never heard of. He reached the end room and went inside.

American George came over and patted Ray on the back. Ray my man, how you doing? This is my partner Nicolaas. He gestured over to the grey-haired man sitting behind a cluttered desk by the meshed window.

Nicolaas stood, leaned across the desk and offered his hand. Pleased to meet you Ray.

Ray shook and looked around the room. A year planner on the wall, a grey metal filing cabinet, a shelf full of videos. He stood in front of the desk looking across at Nicolaas. No time for bullshit. Straight in and get out. He took the jar out of his pocket and put it on the desk. Okay. Let's do it. This is it. You know my terms. Just hand over the money and the keys and I'll be moving. As long as I get the rest of the money in Dover we won't need to speak again.

Nicolaas took the jar and held it up to the light. Squinting like

<212>

he was checking an expensive gemstone. He swilled the liquid around, looked at Ray's distorted face through a blue tinted vortex and smiled.

Ray lit a cigarette and waited.

Okay Ray. We'll buy it. We'll trust you. Nicolaas put down the jar and told George to take Ray through into the next room to get the money.

The adjoining room was bigger than the office space but with even less furniture. A pair of wooden chairs leaned against the wall under the boarded-over window. To the right of the chairs was a large grey metal cupboard. George handed Ray a small key and told him to go and open the cupboard. It's in there Ray. Help yourself.

The key slid in and Ray turned the lock. He felt something bang against the door. Something heavy. He took a step backwards as the door opened and Lisa tumbled out onto the carpet. She was bound up with silver ducting tape, wrapped around her body, arms behind her back. Another strip covered her mouth and Ray couldn't hear what she was saying. Her hair was matted across her face with a mixture of sweat and blood that had seeped from a raised cut above her left eye. Ray bent over her. Looked into her eyes. You cunts. He turned to face American George. You fucking cunts. George and Nicolaas stood smiling with their arms folded. Next to them stood another man with a blond crewcut, holding a chrome finish .38. And walking through the doorway behind them all was Rudi. His face cracked by a wide brown-toothed grin. Shark smile. Teeth. Click. Click. Click.

Hello Ray. You finally made it.

Nicolaas walked over to Ray and told him to sit down on one of the chairs. American George took a roll of ducting tape from a shelf inside the metal cupboard and started wrapping it around Ray. Tight across his body, around the chair. He struggled. Kicked

<213>

out his legs. Rudi sauntered over and punched him in the face and then chuckled as he rubbed his knuckles. Lisa lay there, unable to move, struggling to shout something against the gag. Eyes staring up at Ray. Pleading with him. Asking him. Ray felt the gun at his temple. Frozen. He couldn't move. A trickle of blood ran from his nose into his mouth. He ran his tongue over a chipped tooth and spat out blood.

He looked at Lisa. Baby, I'm sorry. Jesus. I'm sorry.

American George had finished up with the tape and Ray was wrapped tight into the chair. Arms stuck by his side. Feet bound to the chair legs. Nicolaas hauled Lisa up and sat her on the other chair then American George got more tape and wrapped her up tight.

Rudi was leaning against the door frame, his bulk blocking out the light from behind him like an eclipse. A menthol cigarette grasped in his fat baby fingers. Ray, I said it. I told you not to fuck me around. We could've done something together. Only you had too much up here. He tapped the top of his head. Too fucking much. You think too much Ray. You're a dreamer. He stepped forward and stubbed the cigarette out on Ray's forehead, turned, slapped Lisa across the face with the back of his hand and leaned back against the wall and yawned. Started picking at his finger nails.

Ray started shaking the chair. Lifting it up, banging it down on the floor. Okay man. Do what you want to me. Any fucking thing you want to do but let Lisa go. She didn't do anything. She had nothing to do with any of it.

Lisa was moaning, shouting against the gag. Louder now. Nicolaas walked over to her and tore off the strip of tape from her mouth with a sound like ripping sheets. She screamed loud. The sound bounced around the room, echoing. Fuck you. Screaming at Nicolaas, at American George. Staring at the man from the Mercedes who was leaning over her pointing the gun.

<214>

Screaming, Fuck you. Then she turned to Ray and spoke softly. Forget it Ray. I'm not going anywhere. We've got nowhere left to go. I'm staying right here.

Rudi had walked out of the room and came back in carrying the jar. He broke the seal on the top and brought it over to Ray. He held it up to Ray's mouth. Ray turned his head away and Rudi slapped him across the face.

Just a little bit Ray. Try it.

He forced the jar up to Ray's mouth again and tilted it. The liquid dribbled out and over Ray's chin. He spat it out. Rudi hit him again. Hard to the side of the head.

I said drink it. The man with the gun jabbed the barrel into Ray's temple and Rudi tilted the jar. Ray took a mouthful. Held it. He felt the gun tapping him under his chin.

Drink it.

Ray swallowed. Rudi took the jar over to Lisa. Held it up to her. She opened her mouth and let him pour the liquid in. She swallowed then opened her mouth again.

C'mon man, pour it in pour the whole lot in. C'mon.

She opened her mouth wide. Rudi grunted and put the top back on the jar. Okay, Ray we'll be seeing you. He backed out of the room followed by Nicolaas and American George. Footsteps along the corridor, down the steps. Laughing. Distant fading conversation. The blond with the gun took up the space leaning against the door frame.

Ray turned his head and looked at Lisa. She blew him a kiss through swollen lips and he bit his lip. I'm sorry baby. We should never have tried it. We didn't stand a chance. Lisa started to giggle. Oh Ray look at us. Pinned out. Isn't it just the stupidest thing. Lisa started laughing loudly. I love you Ray. I do. She felt the tape around her arms and legs loosen and fall away. The wooden chair became soft like an armchair. Holding her in. Swallowing her. Ray looked over at her as a thousand tiny

<215>

fireworks exploded around the room. Beautiful. Lisa you look
beautiful. Truly.

Ray smiled as he watched the man with the gun turn into
Lisa saw the walls of the room contract. Start pulsing. In and
the shape of a naked cowgirl. A playing card the size of the door
out. The gun dribbled silver, mercury running over
span across the room, disappeared. Loose Joints hobbled over
the floor that was sloping towards her. Hey Ray we nearly
and started cutting the tape away from the chair. No, Lisa first.
made it. A grey cat sleeping in the sunlight. She looked
Lisa first. Looking over at her. She smiled back at him. Loose
over at him. Lips parted. Kiss me Ray. Fuck me Ray. The
Joints shrank away until he disappeared through a crack in the
floor fading out. Falling. Blue skies. Falling. Reaching out
floor. Sucked down. Chased by a fat blue shark. The room spun
her hand. Touching Ray. Falling. Seeing distant green and grey
like it was caught in a whirlpool. Liquid air picking up chairs,
coming up. Faster. Wind blowing her hair. We're going to make
sucking them through the crack in the floor. Out in the sky and
it. Holding him tight. Falling. Ground coming faster. Streets, they
fell like rain. Lisa trapped in a glistening droplet. Pushing
bridges, canals. Houses, cars, boats, people. Ray we're going to
his hands up against the clear wet walls. Trying to reach out to
make it. Faces pressed together. Leaves brush against her face.
her. Falling faster. A gust of wind blows them together. The two
Inches now. Wings burst from her back. She holds him tight
droplets merge and they hit the ocean
and they start to soar.

<216>

Baby, You're Dynamite

Queen Jane Approximately and Absolutely Sweet Marie were seated in a small screening room watching the end titles roll on the film that they'd finished making ten days earlier. A few of the cast and crew sat yawning in their seats, most having declined the invitation to another low rent premiere. The rest of the seats were taken by a similarly poor turnout of actors and actresses from the film that had shown earlier. A handful of representatives from film and video distribution companies talked their way through both pictures, barely looking up at the screen at all. The directors of both films and Nicolaas and American George had sat at the back shouting their approval as each scene played out. Jane giggled and squeezed Marie's arm as her name came up on the credits, filling the whole screen while a Bob Dylan soundalike sang Lay Lady Lay *on the soundtrack. I don't believe it Marie. We made it. Look at that. My name up there. The name dissolved, replaced by more names, smaller this time, three in a row. Look. Look. Your name too. Oh, they spelt it wrong. Maria? Oh well everybody'll know it's you. It doesn't matter.*

The lights came up in the theatre and Jane and Marie climbed out of their seats and went up to meet with George and Nicolaas.

Baby you're dynamite. A natural.

You too Marie. You've got it if you want it.

That scene with the icicle. Wow. Hot enough to melt the fucking film. Genius touch. Incredible.

While the rest of the audience filed out to the reception area American George introduced Jane to a stooped man dressed in a plain blue suit. This is my friend Steve Bachin. He's over from New York. He dug the picture Jane. He's going to take it up. Distribution right across the USA.

Jane smiled and shook Bachin's outstretched hand.

<217>

Listen Jane, I've been talking to Nick and we want you to make some more movies for us. You too Marie. Come over to the office and we'll talk. You got a future here. Really. You got it made.

Jane and Marie followed the men out into the reception room. Thirty or so people stood around drinking white wine and talking. People were coming up to George and Nicolaas shaking their hands saying, Great movies guys, another couple of winners.

Jane reached for a glass of wine and started drinking. Marie looked around at the people laughing and congratulating one another. American George and Nicolaas had disappeared across the other side of the room. Marie stood next to Jane. Nobody came over to talk to them. Nobody seemed to even notice that they were there.

<218>

Born in 1966, Kirk Lake left school at 16 and has worked in a variety of crap jobs. He has released 2 albums of spoken word/music and has worked with the Boo Radleys, Tindersticks, Sonic Boom and others. _Never Hit The Ground_ is his first novel.

ORDER FORM

PULP BOOKS

Call Me	P-P Hartnett	£7.99
Come	Mark Waugh	£8.99
Come + CD	feat. Anti@lias/Overcoat	£11.99
Never Hit The Ground	Kirk Lake	£10.00
Pass Go	Simon Lewis	£10.00
Their Heads Are Anonymous	Alistair Gentry	£8.99

PULP FACTION fiction compilations

5 Uneasy pieces	Cotton, Penrake, Hilaire, McGregor, Tookey	£7.50
Allnighter	Iain Sinclair, Nicholas Blincoe...	£7.50
Random Factor	Jeff Noon, Steve Aylett, Vicky Grut...	£7.50
Fission	Eroica Mildmay, Alistair Gentry...	£6.99
Technopagan	Jeff Noon, Simon Lewis, Scanner...	£6.99
The Living Room	Deborah Levy, Joe Ambrose, Adam j Maynard...	£6.99
Skin	Barry Adamson, Bertie Marshall...	£5.99

Subtotal	

free in the UK
£1 per book Europe
£2 per book rest of world (airmail)

➕ **Postage**	

Orders of 2 books or more deduct £2

➖ **Multibuy**	

Name _____

Address _____

_____

I enclose a cheque payable to PULP FACTION for £

TOTAL

Send to: **PULP FACTION,** PO Box 12171, London N19 3HB